APACHE AMBUSH

STONECROFT SAGA 15

B.N. RUNDELL

Apache Ambush

Paperback Edition

Wolfpack Publishing
5130 S. Fort Apache Road 215-380
Las Vegas, NV 89148

wolfpackpublishing.com

Paperback ISBN 978-1-64734-558-7
eBook ISBN 978-1-64734-556-3

APACHE AMBUSH

DEDICATION

To my characters, Gabe, and Ezra, whom I have come to know as well as my own brothers. I have grown with them, traveled, and fought with them, and learned with them. It has been an exciting and interesting journey to take and many have joined us on the way. For that, I am very grateful. And as you, the reader, have come to know them and grow with them, I trust you will take a bit of them with you as you journey onward. May you go with God.

1 / REFLECTIONS

The two bighorn rams collided, the strike of horns sounding like the boom of a boulder crashing down from a high precipice and splitting at the impact. The racketing sound echoed across the canyon, bouncing off the limestone cliffs and returning to the white chalk-like cliffs on the north side. The muscular rams stood apart, shaking their heads yet never taking their eyes off their opponent. They stepped backwards, looking as if they were in a cadence of unison, each step measured and calculated, until they stopped, shaking their heads again. The animals, both mature males with horns that made more than a full curl, slowly lifted to stand erect, front feet pawing at the air, stretched to their full height. They leaned forward into the charge, then dove toward one another with three lunging steps until they collided again with an impact that resounded through the canyon, yet neither one making a grunt nor a sound as they stood immobile, staring at one another. Until one looked away, took two tentative steps and glanced back over his shoulder at the other ram, now standing with head hanging, and walked away toward the waiting herd. The second ram soon followed, for this was not a battle for dominance and mastery of the herd; this was spring time and the beginning of practice jousts among the big rams.

Gabe sat on the porch, coffee steaming from the cup at his side, and lowered the brass tube telescope, a grin splitting his face as he glanced to Ezra, his life-long friend and brother in every way but blood. "Ain't they somethin'?"

Ezra chuckled, "Ain't nuthin' I ain't seen before," he casually remarked, sipping at his coffee. "I used to watch you do that all the time! Every time you got flustered and mad at yourself for some dumb stunt you'd done, you'd walk up to that big ol' oak tree and bang your head against it so hard I thought one day it'd topple over!"

"I did not!"

"You did so! And you know you did, unless of course you knocked any remembrance of it right outta that pea brain of your'n."

Both men laughed at the memory as Gabe re-cased the scope and took up his coffee cup. He shook his head as he looked at his friend, "Seems like a hundred years ago."

"Ah, not so long. It's been what, now, eight years?"

"Yeah, thereabouts. Lot has happened in that time though. Remember when we used to run through the woods outside of Philadelphia, hunting squirrels and rabbits, pretending they were Redcoats and buffalo?" He glanced at a grinning Ezra and continued, "Those were the days, not a care in the world."

"Yeah, and I remember when you wanted to let loose that pet squirrel in my father's church! Can you imagine what that woulda done to those folks," he chuckled as he pictured the crowd in his father's church, the Mother Bethel African Methodist Episcopal Church, "I knew if we did that, my father'd catch us and skin us alive!"

"Mighta been worth it!" laughed Gabe, remembering.

"Not hardly, but I also remember you wouldn't even consider letting it loose in Christ Church!"

"Are you kidding? They were so stuffy, if anybody dared smile or laugh, the pastor would probably have a hissyfit! And if a squirrel got loose in there . . . hehehe . . . I could just see ol' Ben Franklin havin' apoplexy!" chuckled Gabe, shaking his head.

The men fell silent for a few moments, remembering their youth and the many escapades since, as they journeyed across the continent to the wilderness of Spanish Louisiana and the mountains of the west. In their journeys over the last several years, they had visited and befriended many different native peoples from those along the Ohio River, across the plains, and in the vast Rocky Mountains. They had explored, discovered, and learned so many things, but they had long ago resolved to never lose that spirit of discovery.

Ezra looked at his friend, watching him as he squirmed and twisted in the chair, frowning as he stared into the distance across the valley below them and to the mountains that rose behind them and across the wide river valley to the east. Ezra grinned, "Gettin' it, ain'tcha'!?"

Gabe looked at Ezra, frowning, "Gettin' what?"

Ezra huffed, shook his head, "What? You know what, the wanderlust is what!"

Gabe shook his head, tried to settle back into his chair and finished off the coffee, tossed the dregs over the porch rail into the flower bed and looked back at Ezra, "Reckon."

"So, what'cha wanna do?"

Gabe just stared off the porch, breathing deep, then turned to look at Ezra, "I dunno. I've thought about this country to the west of these mountains," nodding to the towering Sawatch Range of peaks that stood with their heads in the clouds behind them, "cuz we haven't spent much time a'tall looking on the west slope of the mountains. Then there's those mountains over that'away," pointing to the south with his chin. "The Sangre de Cristo Mountains stretch to the south quite a ways, accordin' to what White Knife said."

"Ummhmm, and them Comanche oughta know. That is their country but didn't he say the Ute are on the west side o' them mountains?"

"And the Jicarilla Apache to the south," added Gabe.

"Those Comanchero you traded with summer 'fore last, weren't they from the south?"

"Yeah, they were. White Knife said they were from the Santa Fe area."

"So, if we was to go to Santa Fe, there'd be places we could do some tradin' and resupply? And maybe find out what's happenin' back home?" suggested Ezra, cocking one eyebrow up in a question.

Gabe grinned, slowly nodding, "Yup, prob'ly. And if we took the long way around, we'd see some different country!"

Ezra leaned forward, "Look, we been here longer'n we been anywhere. We spent three winters, two summers, and now we're startin' into our third spring. The young'uns are growin' like weeds and we been wantin' to get some weapons for 'em, and we need some supplies. Dove said we're gettin' almighty low on coffee, we're outta sugar, salt, and I don't know what all. So, I'm thinkin' we need to get the horses some exercise!"

Gabe grinned, leaned forward and rested his elbows on his knees, looked at Ezra, "But, here's the big question. If we do, does everybody go?"

"That, my friend, is a question that I can't answer. Dast we put that question to the ladies?"

"Prob'ly the only safe way," resolved a grinning Gabe as the two men stood to go into the cabin and discuss these things with the womenfolk.

Cougar Woman, a proven warrior and war leader of the Tukkutikka Shoshone, became Gabe's wife shortly after they met en route to the Shoshone grand encampment. They had two sons, Bobcat, age five, whose eastern name was after his father, Gabriel, and Fox, age four, whose eastern name was after Gabe's father, Boettcher.

Grey Dove, also a proven warrior, was a member of the Kuccuntikkka Shoshone. She and Ezra had two children, Chipmunk, age six, whose eastern name was Ezekiel, after Ezra's father, and Squirrel, age four, whose eastern name was Colleen, after Ezra's mother.

The two families were more like one extended family. Although the women were not sisters, though Gabe's first wife who had been killed, was the sister of Dove, they thought of each other as such, and even the children thought of each other as siblings.

When Gabe and Ezra walked into the cabin, the women were finishing up preparations for breakfast and the children were playing together in the corner on the buffalo robes. The women looked up, glanced to one another, and shook their heads. Gabe looked at Ezra, "Why is it they always know even before we do?"

"That my friend, is one of the many mysteries about women that we will never understand," chuckled Ezra as the men took their places at the table.

2 / MOUNTAINS

They held the embrace a little longer than usual, leaned apart and smiled, kissed, and stepped apart. There were no admonitions to 'be careful', 'hurry back', or 'I'll miss you,' for those thoughts were already understood as was the sentiment of love. Both Cougar Woman and Grey Dove knew their men were born to wander but they also knew they would return, for they were confident in the abilities and commitment of their husbands. But Cougar knew also that somewhere and somehow, they would become involved in a situation that would require a fight or more, probably to deliver someone they did not know from some terrible occurrence. It was as certain as the rising of the sun, for that was the way of her man and his friend. They would never fail to help those in need.

The women stepped back as the men swung aboard their mounts, the tall blonde, broad-shouldered, lean

Gabe on his black Andalusian stallion named Ebony, and the shorter, deep-chested and broad-shouldered Ezra aboard his long-legged bay gelding. The big dapple-grey gelding packhorse would trail behind the black, probably free rein as was the habit, while the mule would be the pack animal behind Ezra's bay. The men were typically armed, Gabe with his .62 caliber Ferguson breech-loading flintlock, a matched pair of French double-barreled over/under saddle pistols, a Bailes over/under swivel barrel belt pistol, and his favorite weapon, the cased Mongol bow with a quiver of arrows. Between his shoulder blades hung a brace of Flemish knives, and in his belt a steel-bladed tomahawk.

Ezra sported a Lancaster rifle in the scabbard beneath his right leg, a Bailes belt pistol like Gabe's, and a solitary saddle pistol, a .54 caliber flinter. His preferred weapon was his ironwood war club with the halberd blade that hung at his back, the handle protruding into the air behind his head, handy for Ezra's reach.

With a nod and a smile for the women and a wave to the children, the two friends rode from the clearing before the cabin. The big black Wolf, their constant companion since he was a pup, was in the lead and scouting ahead, anxious to be on the trail. They started west into the deep gorge between the towering granite-tipped and snow-capped mountains. They had made a guess that it would take about two weeks to get to Santa Fe, a week there and two more on the return. Allowing an extra week or two, they expected to return mid-summer. They both twisted in their saddles to turn back for one more glimpse of their families and disappeared into the thick stand of spruce and fir.

Long shadows stretched before them, the rising sun warming their backs, as they took to the familiar trail that hung on the steep shoulder of the south face of the mountains. Below them, meandering through the narrow valley bottom, the creek that carried the spring runoff was cascading over the rocks, running full and crowding the willow-lined banks. It was a familiar trail to them both, having traveled it on their many hunting trips to the high country. The clatter of hooves on loose stones echoed across the narrow gorge, the sound bouncing back as it warned the denizens of the wilderness of their approach.

Gabe breathed deep of the crisp mountain air, reveling in the majestic scenery that surrounded them. Aspen were starting to bud and would soon burst out in pale green leaves that would dance in the slightest breeze, earning the white-barked trees the nickname of quakies. Drifts and deep hollows of snow that hid in the shadows illumined the nooks and crannies of the rugged rocky mountains, waiting their turn to feed the narrow run-off creeks to cascade from the high peaks to the low valley streams.

Both men, ever watchful for any sign of life or danger, were pleased at the sight of a small herd of bighorn sheep moving single file down a steep trail that was seen only by the sure-footed mountain sheep. Below them, noses in the water were several white-rumped mule deer, showing the pale rears to the passerby, unconcerned with them and sure of their ability to escape almost any danger. But a lone buck, with nothing more than velvet-covered stubs for antlers, watched the riders as they passed. A fluffy-coated red fox stopped and stared, one foot lifted, unmoving, as he scanned the newcomers.

The men traveled in silence, taking in the majesty of God's creation all around them, enjoying the wildlife and the clear mountain air. They pulled their capotes tight around them, the temperature dropping lower the higher they climbed. The horses' breaths were seen as they plodded on the path, leaving white flecks of frost around their nostrils.

It was pushing mid-day when they approached the confluence of runoff streams and the dividing of the valleys. Gabe chose a sun-warmed, grassy clearing near the stream that still showed ice along the banks and stepped down. He looked to Ezra, "A cup of hot coffee would taste almighty good 'bout now, don'tcha think?"

"You don't hafta ask me twice!" declared Ezra as he swung his leg over the rump of the big bay. He grabbed a handful of smoked meat from the parfleche as Gabe started for the stream, coffee pot in hand. They soon had the small hat-sized fire blazing, coffee pot dancing alongside, as they found a couple of warm flat rocks for seats. Gabe stroked Wolf's scruff, looked around, "Right about here is where I saw that silver-tip grizz the first time."

"You mean the one we tangled with and is now the kid's play rug?"

"Ummhmm, that's the one. He reared up right over there," pointing with his chin, "and snarled at me but when he saw Wolf at my side, he apparently had second thoughts and rambled off to them trees yonder."

Ezra looked around, his eyes taking in the tall peaks on either side of the long narrow valley below them, shook his head, "Sure is mighty purty country."

"Yup. Sure 'nuff. God musta had himself a time creatin' all this and I can just see him standin' back, hands on his hips and declaring, 'It is good!'"

"Ummhmmm, but right now that coffee is smellin' mighty good, so I think we need to pour a cup!" declared Ezra, reaching for the pot. He looked at Gabe as he poured a cup and asked, "So, which way we goin' from here?" He nodded toward the valley that bore to the south, "That way," and turned to point to the west with his chin, "or that way?"

Gabe chuckled, "I was lookin' both ways when we came into the open and I think we'll take this south branch. That ridge at the end of this long cut, even though there's a trail from here, I think that ridge has too much snow to cross. This way probably has snow also but hopefully there'll be a little easier crossing. I think that'll put us on the western edge of the mountains, a little lower country, less snow, and hopefully easy goin'."

They started up the south valley as the trail crossed the bald face of the left shoulder. The valley made a wide westerly bend and the trail took to black timber. Within a short distance, the shaded snow deepened and Ebony was breaking trail in drifts that were often belly deep. When a break in the timber offered a view of the valley floor, Gabe nudged Ebony down the slope to the side of the narrow creek on the south-facing slope. The bald slope offered a clear trail and warm sunshine. Wolf trotted far ahead, affording Gabe occasional glimpses of the black fur as he darted in and out of the oak brush and creek-side willows. But the valley narrowed, taking a northerly bend and the timber soon crowded the creek, giving shade and cold to the riders. But the timber soon gave way revealing the long talus ridge that stood above timberline and sided the valley on the east for about two miles. The only timber was the bristlecone pine, stunted scraggly pine that leaned away from the cold wind that blasted the trees, turning the wind facing bark an embarrassed red. The trail made a switch back to round a timber-covered knob and turn again to a saddle crossing between two peaks.

Gabe stopped, looking up at the trail that disappeared under a wide swath of snow that lay across the saddle like a thick blanket. The cold air whistled against his face, prompting him to pull the collar of the capote around his neck and tug at the brim of his floppy felt hat. The biting cold felt like needles piercing his exposed skin. He squinted his eyes against the cold, tears escaping from the corners, as he searched the slope, wondering if they could cross. Ezra reined up beside him, holding his capote tight at his throat, "Don't look good!" he said, raising his voice to be heard over the whistling wind.

"I think we'll go up there to that cut back, then I'll check it out on foot!" declared Gabe, nodding to the trail that scarred the bald rocky face of the saddle.

"Your neck!" answered Ezra, knowing it would be a waste of words to try to talk his friend out of his proposed endeavor.

Gabe dug heels to the black's ribs and started up the trail. As the trail bent back on itself once it came from the timber, they were on the lee side of the mountain and the wind lessened. But there was nothing to offer any other protection, the rock face and altitude were prohibitive to any living thing, except a yellow-bellied marmot that stood on hind legs, buck teeth showing, as he watched the strange visitors to his domain.

Gabe stepped down, handed the reins to the black to Ezra, and with his head down, started up the remainder of the trail that disappeared into the frozen tundra. He went to hands and knees as he started up the face of the glacier, clawing his way up the first part until he was able to stand erect. He searched the slope, leaned into the wind that whipped over the saddle crossing, and trudged forward. The snow was hard packed, crusted, and frozen. It easily supported his weight but he was uncertain about the horses. The granular surface crunched underfoot, his feet sliding a little with every step, and he dropped to hands and knees to climb to the crest.

On the left of the saddle, the wind had blown the slide rock free of snow, the sun finishing the task. Before him, the glacier-like snow was almost a mirror image of that he had just climbed but he could see the far edge and the tree-lined valley beyond. If they could make it that far, there would be a decent campsite for the night, sheltered and good firewood. The thought of a warm fire encouraged Gabe as he turned back to Ezra and the horses. He walked and slid down the glacier face, went to Ezra's side and turned to face the glacier as he explained his plan.

"If we lead the horses up there," pointing to the far edge where the glacier tapered, "I think we can lead them over the saddle and down the other side. I think it'll hold 'em but there's only one way to find out. It ain't gonna be easy. But there's a good campsite on the other side with a good place for a fire."

"Now, that's the only thing you've said that I like!" declared Ezra as he swung down from his saddle.

3 / CROSSING

"How 'bout I take the mule for the first over?" suggested Ezra as Gabe turned to look back up the steep slope.

Gabe turned back to Ezra, glanced up at the sun off his right shoulder, "We've got time, if we don't run into too much trouble, and might even make it over the next ridge."

"The next ridge?!" asked Ezra, incredulously, narrowing his eyes as he looked at Gabe.

Gabe chuckled, "Yeah, it looks to be 'bout like this 'un. Over the top here," nodding to the saddle crossing above them, "there is just the headwater of the runoff creek that cuts a swath down the mountain. The next ridge appears to mark the beginning of a long draw that goes to the flat country further down." He paused, looked at Ezra again, "But I like your idea of using the mule first. He is a little more surefooted than the horses."

Ezra shook his head as he reached for the lead rope of the mule and without any further comment, started to the edge of the glacier. He left the trail to move to the right just below the edge of the big sheet of ice, crossed a rocky moss-covered hump and stepped around a low-growing cluster of Alpine Forget-me-nots that were showing blue buds anxious for summer's sun. A smaller patch of moss campion that was showing tiny star-like purple flowers added to Ezra's amazement at the high-altitude greenery in the cold winds of spring. As he neared the flat edge of the ice, he gingerly stepped up, his moccasins doing little to stay the cold, and took several steps as he stretched out the lead line. He stopped, turned to face the recalcitrant mule, and spoke, "C'mon mule," as he tentatively pulled on the lead rope. The long-eared beast lay his ears back and stretched out his neck but didn't move. "C'mon mule, you can do it! Let's show Gabe what you can do!" Ezra was certain the big brown jack rolled his eyes in the direction of Gabe, then took a step onto the dirty snowpack. The crust crunched, but did not give way, and one hoof was joined by another and the rear hooves joined the rest.

Ezra turned uphill, rope held taut at his side, and tested each step before trusting it with his weight. The mule was wide-eyed, head and neck stretched out, as he carefully took step after step. The pair had made about thirty feet when Ezra lost his footing and fell to one knee but the crust held and he regained his feet and continued. The mule appeared to be tiptoeing as he dug in the front edge of his hooves with each step. Ezra angled across the face of the glacier until he neared the far-left rim of the dirty snow at the edge of the talus; he turned to move across the remaining distance at an angle that would reach the crest at the far edge. It was evident the glacier was like a dirty white blanket that lay over the saddle crossing between the two buttes that marked the mountain pass but it also was open to the daylight and the afternoon sun was showing its worth as the snow underfoot began to feel a little spongy.

Ezra kept his eyes on the crest, feeling his way with his sodden moccasined feet. Even though these were his high-topped winter moc's and were lined with rabbit fur, the mutton tallow made from the rendered fat of the bighorn sheep was helpful, but the icy melt still found its way through the buffalo hide bottoms and elk hide tops. He was within twenty feet of the crest when he heard the mule flounder and the lead rope draw tight, almost pulling him over backwards. He dropped to one knee, slipped a shoulder under the lead and looked back to see the mule fighting to free one leg from a crumpled edged hole in the snow. The mule used Ezra as an anchor and came to his feet, stood shaking a moment, then stepped out to follow

Ezra. The mule moved around the hole, carefully testing each step. With unsure footing and a slip or two, he made the crest beside Ezra.

The south-facing slope had done a better job of melting off and their descent through the crumbled and soft snow was easier and more quickly accomplished. Once free of the ice field, Ezra ground tied the mule and started back up the slope. When he cleared the crest, he was surprised to see Gabe leading the horses, one trailing after the next, the reins of the bay tied to the tail of Ebony, and the grey doing his usual following sans lead. They were spaced out about eight feet apart and were approaching the turnback at the far edge when Ezra stood, hands on hips, at the crest, watching.

Ezra cupped his hands to his mouth and hollered down, "When you near that hole, take the low side, it's firmer!"

Gabe waved his free hand, sent Wolf ahead, made the switchback and started toward Ezra. Ebony moved close behind Gabe, confident in his friend and rider, but the bay resisted the lead, pulling back and tossing his head. As they neared the hole made by the mule, Gabe stepped to the downhill side, careful with each step, and led the two horses wide of the hole and both had secure footing. But the grey, strong minded as he was, charged straight through the crunched and scattered depression. What footing there had been, soon gave way and he suddenly found himself belly deep in snow and ice. He stood stock still and Gabe turned to holler at Ezra but he saw his friend already coming to the downed horse.

"Keep on goin'! I'll get him. Get those two up top!" Ezra spouted as he passed by Gabe.

Gabe leaned into the lead rope on Ebony's headstall and trudged the rest of the way to the crest. Once atop the slope, he dropped the lead line to ground tie the horses and started slipping and sliding back down the gravelly ice-covered slope. Ezra stood beside the head of the grey, stroking his head and neck, calming him down until Gabe came alongside and dug a long hemp rope from the pack. He looped it around the rump of the grey, walked to the front and handed the rope to Ezra. "You take this and when we're ready, you lean into it with all you got. I'll use the lead line and pull on the halter, that'll give him an anchor and you pullin' on his rear will help his footing."

Gabe loosed the lead rope that usually hung around the grey's neck in a loop, stretched out in front of the horse and dug in his feet. "C'mon boy, give it a try," and leaned back with all his weight. "Now, Ezra, pull!" The grey stretched out his head and neck, and when he felt the pull on his rump and the taut lead rope, he started kicking out with his front feet, pawing for footing. One foot found a hold and he came up from the snow a few inches, then the second foot caught something solid and he moved more. With a big kick from his rear, he lunged forward, fought for footing, and came from the loose snow and crashed through the crust of the glacier again. With continued tries, he found better footing and rose atop the icy crust. He stood trembling, fearful of falling through, as he looked at both Gabe and Ezra who had fallen on their backs when his feet caught hold and gave sudden slack to the ropes.

Both men were laughing, breathing hard of the thin high-altitude air, and finally rolled to their bellies to come to all fours and finally stand up. Gabe reached back to stroke the grey's head, picked up the lead line and said, "C'mon boy, we can do it," and started to the crest. Once on top, they stopped to catch their breath, then Ezra took the bay and started to the mule. Within a short while, they were below the icy crest and approaching the bristlecone pines at trail's edge. Ezra looked at the trail ahead, where it cut through the trees and took to the steep slide rock slope before passing under an overhang of rimrock just below the next saddle crossing. He turned to look at Gabe, "Well, doesn't look like there's much snow over there but that trail don't look much wider'n an eyebrow!"

Gabe grinned, looked at the sun that was now off their right shoulder, "But I think we can make it 'fore dark easy 'nuff. Don't you?"

"As long as we stick to the trail and don't try any

shortcuts!" answered Ezra, nodding toward the grey.

"Well, I think I'll keep him on his lead line, leastways till we get over that ridge yonder."

"Suits me! Since I think I'm gonna take the lead anyhow!" answered Ezra as he stepped aboard the bay and bent down to grab the mule's lead line. Gabe chuckled as he coiled the hemp rump rope and stashed it in the pannier. He picked up the lead of the grey and swung aboard Ebony, motioned to Wolf to take the trail, and started out after Ezra.

They were in the horseshoe upper end of a long draw that dropped from the high country into the black forests below. The trail bent above timberline to cross the slide rock talus ridge. Slide rock is so called because it is found in a large slide area below a higher mountain top and is composed of flat rock, about two to four inches thick, usually covered with lichen and moss on one side, and few pieces larger than a saddle blanket, with most being roughly eighteen inches by twenty-four, all irregular shaped and lying loosely balanced on the rocks beneath. The trail was made up of crushed rock, blown in dirt and dust, and trampled vegetation and usually no more than eighteen to thirty inches wide.

Gabe watched as Ezra let the bay have his head and pick his own footing. The mule appeared totally unconcerned and even bored with the trek but the horses were a little more apprehensive, heads down, picking their steps, choosing each move. They slowly worked their way across the slide rock without incident, made the horseshoe bend to the narrower part of the trail and Gabe chuckled silently as he remembered Ezra's description of this as an 'eyebrow' trail, thinking that might have been an exaggeration. The trail made a steady incline toward the saddle yet just before the crest, they had to pass under an overhang from the rimrock that shadowed the trail.

The only sound to be heard was the clatter of hooves on the rocky path or an occasional snort of the horses or mule. Both Gabe and Ezra were silent and breathing slowly as they looked from the trail to the shear drop off that fell away some three hundred feet or more to the trees below. Gabe caught movement and looked below to see a golden eagle soaring on updrafts and shook his head at the thought they were so high they were looking down on the wide wings of the eagle and listened as he squawked his cry.

Gabe's attention was quickly brought back to the rocks that hung above them when a rock slipped its mooring and tumbled over the point of rocks overhead. Smaller pebbles rattled free and bounced to the trail as the bigger rock hit the trail, and bounced over the edge, crashing over the slide rock below to smash into the treetops. The rock hit the trail just behind the mule, spooking it to lunge forward and smack into the back of the bay, who, startled, kicked back at the mule, eliciting a loud braying from the long-eared beast and a skittish jumping about of both.

Gabe pulled down on the reins of the black, taking a deep seat just in case, and dallied the lead rope of the grey as he pulled it tight. But all Ebony did was a slight side step as he tried to toss his head but the taut hold of Gabe held him secure and he stopped fidgeting. The grey took his cue from the black and rested his chin on the rump of the black as they watched the tussle with the bay and mule.

Ezra, startled when the mule bumped against his bay, had taken a tight grip on the rein and pulled the bay's nose to his chest as he dallied the lead of the mule to the saddle horn. But the two animals were still bumping and shoving, unknowing what was happening when the rocks tumbled down and Ezra dug heels to the bay, giving him something to do. The gelding lunged forward, the crest of the saddle crossing in sight and took the rest of the trail at a canter, dragging the mule behind, braying, and pulling on the lead, dragging his heels in protest. Once at the crest, Ezra reined up and reached down to stroke the bay's neck and talked to him, trying to settle him down and keeping the lead on the mule as short as possible.

When Ezra took off, Gabe made a quick glance up at the rock and quickly decided Ezra had the right idea and dug heels to Ebony to follow after his friend. They reined up beside Ezra and Gabe stepped down, needing solid ground beneath his feet as he tried to slow his own heartbeat and breathing. The men chuckled as they looked at one another and Gabe said, "That ain't no trail to have a horse race!"

4 / SMOKE

By early morning, when the sun was barely bending its lances of light over the high eastern peaks, Gabe and Ezra were following the game trail that shadowed the run-off creek from the high country. The slopes on their left were thick with black timber, tall skinny fir and scattered towering spruce. Several basins and draws held patches of aspen showing the first sign of green. When they rounded a slight point of a ridge, they confronted a sizeable herd of elk grazing in the valley bottom that took flight and stampeded into the timber.

"Now, that's a big herd o' elk!" declared Ezra, having reined up to watch the scampering herd.

"Had to be at least a couple hunnerd!" responded Gabe, shaking his head. "You see those bulls at the back just showin' velvet?"

"They were big 'uns!"

"But were we the only reason they took off?" asked Gabe, standing in his stirrups to look around the valley bottom. He pointed to a break in the timber that carried a small creek, "Uh, mebbe they had somethin' to do with it!"

A big grizzly with two cubs scurrying behind ambled from the break, paused when she got the scent of man and horses, and rose to her hind feet, searching for the source. When she spotted the intruders, she pawed at the air like a boxer in the ring, cocked her head to the side and opened her mouth to let a roar bounce across the valley. She watched Gabe and Ezra for any reaction but, seeing none, she dropped to all fours, looked back at the cubs, grunted, and ambled toward the creek in the valley bottom.

Gabe and Ezra sat watching, stroking the necks of their horses, and talking to them to reassure them and keep them calm, for they had smelled and seen the grizz and were being a little skittish. Gabe snapped his fingers at Wolf, "Easy boy, stay," and motioned him to the side. All the horses and the mule had heads up, ears forward, eyes wide, as they watched the bear family parade across the valley. When they splashed across the creek and split the willows to take to the timber on the far side, Gabe spoke softly, "We'll give 'em a few minutes, then we'll skedaddle on past."

He slipped the Ferguson from the scabbard, checked the load, and lay the weapon across the pommel. With another glance to the trees and the bears, he nudged Ebony forward and the group started on the trail, everyone, horses, and men, watching the trees where the grizzly had disappeared. When they crossed the bear tracks, Wolf stopped and sniffed both ways and, satisfied, trotted on, looking for the next adventure.

Another five miles brought them to a dog-leg bend in the narrow valley as it opened into a wide grassy flat that lay between two ranges of timber-covered foothills. The sun was warm on their shoulders and they shed their capotes, tying them behind the cantles with the bedrolls. As the valley spread wide, they spotted another big elk herd, prompting Gabe to say, "Either that's the same one that found a trail through the trees and beat us here or it's another big 'un!"

"I think it's another'n," drawled Ezra, leaning on his pommel as the bay rolled his shoulders in his long-legged gait. Ezra sat up, looking around, pointed to a patch of white blooming flowers, "Ain't those daisies?" he asked, thinking that most of the early blooming flowers in the mountains were white or yellow. "And them others over there, ain't they those mouse-ear chickweed?"

Gabe frowned, "When did you get so knowledgeable about flowers an' such?"

"Hah! The women, of course, but you had to give me the reg'lar name for 'em. I can't remember what the Shoshone word is for 'em."

Gabe laughed, pointed to a small patch nearby, "And those are lilies and that patch over there is raspberries."

"Too bad those raspberries ain't ripe! I'd like a handful of sweet raspberries 'bout now."

"What's those yellow ones yonder?" asked Gabe, quizzing his friend.

"Look like lilies to me!"

"Yup, those are glacier lilies, see how they're near the edge of the snowdrift in the shade of the trees? The white ones yonder are sego lilies. The white ones, you can eat the bulbs, like the osha. The yellow ones, the leaves make a tea that some natives use to reduce fever and infections."

Ezra frowned and looked at Gabe, "Well, don't you beat all. You're always comin' up with somethin' that amazes me. So, who taught you about that?"

"Who do you think? Cougar Woman, of course."

The men were enjoying the banter as the horses kept up their ground-eating, ambling gait, snatching a mouthful of grass as they walked, the sun warm on their shoulders and the sky without a cloud. Both sides of the valley showed long timbered slopes to the foothills with the many finger ridges on their right coming from the west showing timber on the north faces and bald slopes on the south. The upper reaches of the ridges held thickets of aspen that showed the pale green of early buds. Gabe glanced high above them at the hollows with the thick aspen, knowing that within a few weeks, those vales would show brilliant splotches of green that moved like waves on a lake, the leaves of the aspen quaking in the slightest breeze and always moving.

Wolf was staying close, no more than fifteen to twenty feet ahead of the horses. The group had rounded a slight point, revealing a bend in the valley and more beyond, when Wolf suddenly stopped, head up and ears forward, Ebony also stopped, bringing Gabe and Ezra back to the present. The men frowned as they looked where Wolf pointed with his nose, seeing several thin tendrils of smoke coming from the trees and spiraling into the blue.

"That's gotta be a village," whispered Gabe, frowning.

Ezra chuckled, "What'chu whisperin' for, that's close to two miles away!"

Gabe looked at Ezra, back at the wispy fingers of smoke. "Who do you reckon?"

Ezra shook his head, "Prob'ly the local church havin' a picnic! Who do you think? And just what makes you think I know any more about who that might be than you do?"

Gabe laughed, "All right, all right. Well, we did run into some Spaniards a while back, so it could be somebody besides natives." He frowned, "Didn't Stone Buffalo say all this country was Ute country, just different bands of 'em?"

"Yeah, pretty much. But if I remember right, that was just before the Arapaho came south huntin' buffalo and the Comanche came north, huntin' us!"

Gabe shook his head, chuckling at his friend, "Boy, if you ain't sharper'n a porcupine this mornin'!"

"Cuz I'm gettin' hungry!" he growled.

"So, what do you want to do? Go scratch on one of those lodges and see if you can get one o' those women to fix you sumpin' to eat?"

"Now, there ain't no reason for you to get sassy! I'm just sayin' I'd rather eat than fight!"

Gabe looked around, nodded to a gulch that split two ridges to their right, "There's a little creek comin' from there, let's go up there and have us somethin' to eat and let the horses have a blow while we decide what we're gonna do."

Without a word, Ezra reined the bay away from the trail and took to the draw that had timber on the north-facing slope that offered some shade and the little creek had grassy banks for the horses. A bend around a point would shield them from view of anyone in the valley below and the thick trees would dissipate any smoke from the fire for their coffee.

Once the girths were loosened, the horses were grazing, and the coffeepot was dancing, Gabe took his telescope from the saddlebags and motioned to the top of the hill behind them. "Gonna have a look-see," he stated as he motioned to Wolf to join him. Ezra sat at fireside, watching, and waiting for the coffee as he chewed on some smoked meat. He nodded to Gabe as Gabe started through the scattered trees to climb up the hillside.

As he bellied down and stretched out the scope, Gabe saw the confluence of the stream they followed and another of about the same size and the bigger stream push its way through the foothills to the west. Before him, directly south, a wide stretch of black timbered foothills covered the southern horizon with one prominent draw that climbed the shoulder of the highest mesa before him and another that paralleled the first and crested to the west of the high point. At the base of these foothills, just in the mouth of the second draw, lay the village. Although the lodges were below the crest of the hill at the point that split the two draws, a few tendrils of smoke still showed. With no breeze in the still of the day, the spirals of smoke rose like thin ribbons to dissipate into the clear sky. He could only guess at the size of the village but he knew that if any smoke showed it was because there were several lodges.

He caught movement at the mouth of the first valley, swung his scope, and spotted what appeared to be a hunting party coming from the narrow valley, probably returning to the village. He focused in on the group, saw no sign of war paint, by their appearance, hair, attire, and more, guessed the men to be Ute. The party numbered about fifteen and they trailed several horses, loaded with haunches of meat, probably elk. He watched as they rounded the point and turned into the second valley and rose from his promontory to return to the cookfire with Ezra.

As he walked into the camp, Ezra looked up with a question on his face and Gabe said, "I'm pretty sure they're Ute. I saw a huntin' party of fifteen returnin' to the village but I couldn't see the village to know any more."

"I s'pose you wanna go meet those folks?"

"Dunno. Hafta think on it. But right now, I want some coffee, if you left me any!"

5 / GETAWAY

"Look, there's two draws there, like this," described Gabe, drawing with a stick in the dirt, "and it looks like they both go to the top of the big mesa, here," jabbing the stick in the dirt beyond his scratched map of ravines and such. "Now this draw is where the encampment is but if we take this one, they won't even know we're in the country!" He sat back on the log, reached for his coffee cup, and waited as Ezra looked at his crude lines in the dirt.

Ezra looked up at the sun, over at Gabe, "You think we can just ride across open country and not be seen?"

Gabe chuckled, "If we do it at night!"

"Oh, well, that's different." He looked up at the sun again, "But I think I'd like to go up there," nodding to the hill behind them, "and have a look for my own self."

"We can do that," replied Gabe, reaching for the leather case and the telescope. "C'mon Wolf, let's climb the hill again." He looked to the horses, each one tethered on a long lead, their noses in the grass, and satisfied, he glanced at Ezra, "Well, you comin'?"

At the crest, the two men and Wolf bellied down to survey the countryside. Gabe pointed to the timbered knob of a point that separated the two draws, "That one on the right is where the village lies, the hunting party came from the wider one on the left. That's the way I think we oughta go."

Ezra lifted the scope, stretching it out and focusing on the far hills. He moved it slowly over the point of land, spotted a little smoke on the far side, and centered it on the mouth of the valley. He was searching for any lookouts watching over the camp and looking for any approaching danger. They would usually be on a high point of land, behind cover of some sort, but with their horse or horses nearby. With a scan of the far side, he saw nothing, but the timber was heavy and would easily hide several men. Bringing the scope to bear on the near side and the point or knob of land that split the valleys, he slowly scanned the possible locations. He moved the scope, paused, moved it again, then paused and focused the scope with a twist of the barrel, and slowly grinned as he whispered, "Gotcha!" He lowered the scope and grinned at Gabe, "There's a lookout on that small shoulder of that knob, the one with scattered trees," and handed the scope to Gabe for his confirmation.

"You're right! He wouldn't be so easy to see if he didn't have that paint horse tied behind him."

"Ummhmm, but that horse couldn't be seen from down below where most folks would be if they were comin' at the camp."

"Yup." Gabe had a last look, then handed the scope back to Ezra. "Now, take a good look at that other draw and where we'll probably be goin'."

After a few moments of scoping the route, Ezra spoke with the scope still at his eye, "That's quite a mesa yonder and it looks like from up there a fella'd have a view of the entire southern mountains."

"That's what I was thinkin'. From there it'd be easy to plot our route to Santa Fe."

"Well, seems like it'd be the smart thing, travelin' at night, I mean. That way we'd bypass that camp and any possible problems that would bring. But I reckon they'll have a lookout up there where that'n is, so, we'll have to figger a way past him."

"Look at that arroyo down there in the bottom of the valley," suggested Gabe, pointing below the hilltop to the possible route of their travel. "If we hug this rise there, duck into that arroyo and take the cut yonder, that'll put us almost behind that lookout when we come out on top."

Ezra moved the scope for a close-up look at Gabe's suggested route, moved it along the arroyo and the cut indicated, then to the flat. "I think you're right.

Plus we'll be travelin' at night."

"Yeah, but the moon is 'bout three-quarters, waxing to full, and without any clouds, it'll be pretty bright."

Ezra frowned, "Usually, we're wantin' a full moon so we can travel easy at night but, for tonight, some clouds would be welcome." He tucked the scope back into the case, sat up and looked to the valley bottom, glanced at the sun, and added, "I think I'll get me a little shut-eye 'fore we do this."

Gabe lifted his hands to the sun, stacked them on edge, one atop the other, and calculated, "There's about three hours of daylight till sundown, then 'bout another hour of dusk. So, yeah, a little shut-eye would be welcome." He chuckled and scooted on his rump from the crest of the hill, then stood and followed Ezra through the trees to the camp.

The coyote chorus stirred Wolf awake and his cold nose brought Gabe alert. With a quick glance to the stars, Gabe guessed it to be just past midnight. He stood, stretched, and poked Ezra with his toe to bring him around. Gabe looked around, judging the night light, saw the shadows leaning to the east just a mite and knew the blue of the night was just what they needed. Another look at the sky showed scattered clouds masking the lanterns that dangled high above but there were none near the big moon that smiled down on the dark hills. "Looks 'bout right for us to make our getaway," he said as he started to the stack of gear to ready the horses.

Within a few moments, they started from their camp, down the ravine to the valley below. They had always made certain that every part of their gear and tack was well secured and oiled to prevent any unnecessary noise that could be a giveaway of their presence. But the usual creak of leather on leather, the rattle of hooves on loose stones, and the occasional snort or blow of the horses or mule were things that could not be prevented. Wolf trotted just in front of Ebony often looking back at the horses and riders as they followed and watching for any word or signal from Gabe.

They crossed the creek, the same creek they had followed from the high country earlier, but stayed near the thick willows, moving through the wet grass silently. When he spotted the trickle of a creek that came from the arroyo on his left, Gabe reined Ebony into the mouth of the big arroyo. He let a sigh of relief escape as he relaxed, sitting deep in the saddle when they moved out of sight of any lookout on the far butte. It was about a third of a mile before they came to the cut that would point them to the south and Gabe turned the big black into the narrow defile, moving to the dog-leg bend to the left that was his landmark to climb the high bank and make for the mouth of the valley. He motioned to Ezra and reined up, stepped down, and in soft tones said, "I'm climbin' the bank on foot, don't wanna give ourselves away." He nodded to the big moon, "It's almighty bright, almost like daytime, and we'd easily be seen."

Ezra nodded, accepted Ebony's reins, and watched Gabe start the climb from the arroyo. As he crested the bank, Gabe looked directly toward the promontory that held the lookout and realized they were within a line of sight of his position but there was no way of knowing if he was there or if he was alert enough to see them. Gabe motioned to Ezra and waited as his friend rode across the face of the bank, angling to the top, leading the mule pack animal and the big black trailing the dapple-grey packhorse. As soon as they crested the bank, Gabe swung aboard, "Keep movin', but not too fast!" He looked to the mouth of the valley and the timber-covered hills that sided the meandering creek, judging it to be about a half-mile before they would be out of sight of the lookout.

When anyone is trying to avoid being seen, the temptation is always to duck down, make yourself as small as possible. Gabe felt the need to lie low on Ebony's neck but he knew that effort would be futile. If the lookout would see them, it would be because of the movement of four animals, not the size of the riders. The dark figures moving in the moonlight would be easily seen by an observant lookout. Their only hope was that his attention was focused on the mouth of the valley where the encampment lay or the valley beyond. Gabe shook his head as they moved at a casual walk, aiming for the willows at the edge of the creek coming from the high country at the head of the valley.

Every step seemed to clatter loudly, every creak of saddle leather seemed to squeal into the night, every huff or blow of a horse or mule sounded like a trumpet in the night as the small group moved steadily toward the target creek. The distance seemed interminable, the moonlight too bright, the noise of their movement too loud, and Gabe realized he was holding his breath. He shook his head, took a deep breath, and glanced back at Ezra, grinning. It was too dark to see his expression but Gabe suspected his friend was laughing at their consternation.

Finally, they reached the point where Gabe believed they were beyond the sight of any lookout, at least any that might be where the one had been stationed before, and he stopped to wait for Ezra to come alongside. "I think we're outta sight now, so let's put some distance behind us, what say?"

"Sounds like the thing to do to me!"

Gabe grinned and dug heels to the big black. Ebony lunged forward, drawing the lead of the grey taut, and they started up the valley at a ground eating canter. The grass beside the creek muffled the sound of hoofbeats and the cool night air felt good on their faces.

After about a mile and a half, Gabe pulled the black down to a walk, and the animals blew a little, appreciative of the chance to stretch their legs. Another mile or so and they came to the previously spotted fork in the valley, choosing the fork on the right that bore due south.

Once into the secondary valley beside the smaller creek, Gabe reined up and stepped down. When Ezra neared, Gabe said, "How's about we walk a ways, stretch our legs and give the animals a break?"

Ezra stepped down and followed Gabe as they started up the draw. He looked around, seeing the valley bottom that was about a hundred yards wide, the little chuckling creek cascading over the rocky bottom between the thickets of willows and chokecherries. The hillside on the left was sparse with juniper and piñon, the slope on the right was bald for the first thirty to forty yards, then thick with juniper, some fir and ponderosa that rode the slope to the low crest of the foothills. Before them, the valley narrowed, split, and climbed slowly to the crest of the wide mesa they scoped from the hilltop behind them. They should make it to the top before daylight and would probably stop and have some coffee and maybe something to eat. The thought of coffee and food brought a grin to the man and he quickened his step.

6 / TABEGUACHE

The moonlight lay across the valley, casting dim shadows behind sagebrush and more. Magpie, a young warrior of the *Tabeguache* Ute, was on his first watch, carefully scanning the valley below, searching for anything that might be a danger to the village. For a young man, standing watch was one of the stepping stones to become a full warrior and he was determined to make his family proud. His brown and white paint gelding was tethered behind the clump of juniper and stomped his impatience, prompting Magpie to turn and try to quiet the animal. When he turned back to look at the moonlit valley floor, movement caught his eye and he turned to see four horses, two riders coming from the arroyo and making for the valley beyond the butte. He stood, climbed the rock that had been his refuge, and watched. Two riders, each trailing a packhorse, moved easily into the wide draw below the rise.

They did not appear to be a threat to the village, moving upstream of the small creek and into the wider draw below the butte. But he was directed to report any movement, anyone that was not of the people. He watched as they disappeared below the rise and further up the draw, then turned to give the call of the owl to warn the village. Within moments, the war leader, Walkara, was at his side. He had come silently and startled Magpie as he stepped from the shadows. "Why do you make the cry of the owl?"

"Riders. Two riders, four horses," he turned to point to the valley and the arroyo that cut through the buttes, "they came from there, across the flat and up into that valley."

"Who were they?"

"I could not tell, too dark. But they had strange head coverings," as he made a motion across the top of his head in a flat way to indicate the hats of the men.

"Go," motioning to the village, "bring Blackhawk and another; we will follow these intruders to our land."

The last five miles was through thick timber but the trail was a well-used game trail and showed considerable recent sign of an elk herd that had apparently migrated from the higher mesa into the greener valley below. The trail was wide and easy-traveling. Wolf roved to and fro as he scouted for Gabe and Ezra, catching all the scents of moving game. After reaching the head of the draw, the trail cut diagonally across the face of the mesa, through thick lodgepole pine, but was still easy going. Once they broke from the timber, the expansive panorama showed the blue-tinted countryside basking in the last of the moonlight. The sky had cleared of clouds and the twinkling lanterns of night shone brightly overhead. With a quick look around, Gabe pointed Ebony to the high point, avoiding the bald flat-top and choosing the scattered timber of the crest.

Both horses and men were tired and opted to use the darkness to their advantage and get some shut eye before lighting up the darkness with a campfire. There was ample graze for the animals and they set to the task of snatching up their fair share without delay. The men rolled out their bedrolls under a cluster of skinny fir trees and, within moments, were making the usual sounds of tired men sleeping, snorting, snoring, and mumbling into the darkness.

It seemed like no more than a few minutes until a low growl from the deep chest of Wolf brought Gabe instantly awake. He slowly moved his hand to grasp his saddle pistol that lay beside the saddle he was using as a pillow, moving his head slowly to look in the same direction as Wolf. The thin line of grey told of early morn but the changing of the guard from moonlight to daylight made the shadows appear even darker. A glance to the side showed Ebony looking toward the flat-top of the mesa and Gabe whispered, "You awake?"

"Yeah. See anything?" answered the sleepy Ezra.

"No, but there's somethin'. You and Wolf take to the trees, fluff up your bedroll, and I'll act like nothin's happenin' and make a fire."

Within moments, Ezra's bedroll was empty and Gabe was alone in the small clearing as he gathered up an armload of firewood to start a fire. With the kindling stacked, the tinder below, he used his flint and steel for sparks. He caught a spark, tenderly blew it to life and, as the first flame showed, he fanned it below the kindling to get the fire going. He sat back and glanced at the flames licking at the wood, set the coffee pot on the close-in stone, and listened to the sounds of the early morning.

He heard the approach of soft footsteps, moving quietly through the grass, but the unmistakable sound of buckskin against grass and brush was easily identified by Gabe's experienced ear. He spoke up in Shoshone, suspecting the visitors were Ute and the languages were similar. "You are welcome at my fire. There will be coffee and food soon." He did not look up but kept his eyes averted from the fire, knowing he needed his night vision unimpaired.

"Who are you and why are you here?" came a voice from the darkness.

"I am Spirit Bear, friend to all Ute people. I have been with Stone Buffalo and the *Mouache* Ute, before that with White Raven of the *Yapudttka* Ute. Who are you that comes to my camp? Come close and let me see you."

Two men came into the light of the small fire. The one stepping forward slightly was an impressive figure with a bone hair pipe breastplate, heavy braids falling over his shoulders, a scalp lock dangling to one side and two feathers tucked into a top knot. His broad forehead held thick eyebrows over black eyes, a broad nose, and strong chin. His deep chest rippled under the breastplate and with muscular arms crossed over his chest, he glared at Gabe. "I am Walkara, war chief of the *Tabeguache* Ute people. This is our land and you are intruders."

The second man hung back slightly, a nocked arrow in his bow that he held down before him as he searched the trees for others. Gabe grinned slightly as he stood, motioning to the log opposite the fire, "Join me, I will put some meat on the fire and we can share a meal. You can tell the others to come in from the darkness before my friend decides to kill them for being unfriendly."

Walkara frowned, "There are two of my warriors but one of your friend."

Gabe grinned, "But my friend knows where your warriors are and they know not where my friend waits. And my friend can call the beasts of the woods to his side and take your warriors down before they know they are in danger. But enough talk of death, tell you warriors to come to the fire and we will eat together."

Walkara studied this man before him, glanced to his companion, then lifted his chin as he made the call of the great horned owl to ask questions of the night. Within moments, Gabe mimicked the cry of the nighthawk and the two warriors came from the trees. Seconds later, Ezra and Wolf stepped into the small clearing, startling the Ute warriors at the sight of the black man and the even bigger black wolf. Walkara came to his feet and stepped back as Gabe raised his voice and said, "Walkara of the *Tabeguache* Ute people, this is my friend, Black Buffalo." With a slight hand signal, Wolf came to his side, never taking his eyes off the four Ute, "And this is my friend, Wolf." He motioned to Wolf and the big beast went to his belly beside Gabe, still watching the others.

Gabe sat down, scooped up a handful of fresh ground coffee and dropped it into the pot of hot water, slapped the lid down and turned to Walkara. "We saw you return from a hunt in this valley yesterday. If you're still looking for elk, we saw a sizeable herd up the valley of the other fork of the creek," nodding to the north across the broad valley.

Walkara nodded, "Why are you here?"

"We have a cabin to the north and over the mountains from your village, a good day's travel or more. We are bound for Santa Fe to do some trading, get some supplies."

"You are in the land of the *Tabeguache* Ute, also known as the *Weminuche.* You are going into the land of the *Capote* Ute."

"We have been friends with other bands of the Ute. We spent the winter with Stone Buffalo and the *Mouache.* We would like to be friends with all the Ute people."

As they visited and ate, the Ute often glanced at Ezra and Wolf, curious about both but unwilling to speak about the strange things they saw, a black man and a big wolf that lived with people, these were strange indeed. As they finished their meal, Walkara rose, extended his hand to Gabe and the two men clasped forearms, sealing their friendship. "When you return, if we are still here, stop and meet our people. They would like to see the man that walks with a wolf and a man that is like the buffalo. When we tell them of such things, they will not believe us." He grinned as he glanced from Gabe to Ezra and Wolf. He stepped forward, extended his arm to bid Ezra goodbye, as well, but carefully stepped aside from Wolf. The others looked back repeatedly as they left to retrieve their horses from the trees, probably cautious and concerned about the wolf that might follow. Gabe and Ezra heard them take to the trail aboard their horses and looked at one another, grinning, as Ezra said, "You know, that's the first time we've met other people and didn't have to get in a fight or something because of them. We oughta do that more often!"

7 / CAPUTA

The sun was hidden by the heavy clouds with black bottoms. A cool breeze whispered through the tall pines behind Gabe as he sat, knees up, elbows supporting the extended brass telescope, while he scanned the countryside that lay to the south. Walkara had said that Santa Fe lies due south, just west of the tail end of the Sangre de Cristo Mountains. From his promontory Gabe moved the scope down the long line of pinnacle peaks of the mountain range, snow still painted the mountain tops, but they disappeared in the hazy distance. As he moved the scope to the west, he spoke to Ezra who stood in the shade of the tall ponderosa, "Walkara said that valley," nodding to the south, "is a big 'un, and goes all the way to Santa Fe. He said Santa Fe lies between the mountains and the Rio Grande del Norte or what the Mexicans call Rio Bravo."

"So, we goin' to travel that valley? It looks mighty dry!" asked Ezra, stepping from the shade to look into the distance. "Course, I can't see much from here but what I do see sure ain't green!" He stood spread legged, hand shading his eyes.

"Maybe if we kinda hug these foothills," replied Gabe, pointing to the rolling hills that sided the wide valley on the west, "there'd be plenty of water."

"And Indians too! Didn't Walkara say there's another band of Ute down thataway? What'd he call 'em?"

"Caputa, I think he said." Gabe telescoped in the brass tube and secured it in the leather case. He looked to the distant valley, "It'd be easier travelin' but it also puts us out in the open."

"Yeah, an' I don't like that, unless we travel at night."

Gabe stood, taking another quick glance to the distance, "That might be a good idea. But for now, let's at least get down off this mesa and make it to the edge of that valley for a close-up look."

They dropped off the mesa to the south, picking their way through the timber for a couple of miles before it thinned out, offering several bald slopes and draws that pointed to the arroyo that was their target. It was a creek-bottomed, narrow valley that aimed due south with an easy-going trail that rode the west shoulder. It appeared to be an ancient trail used by more than just game although the only fresh sign was deer. Gabe frowned, reined up, and stepped down. He walked to the rocky slope beside the trail and went to one knee to examine a stack of rocks. He looked at the stones, frowning, glancing to either side and down the trail.

"Is that a cairn?" asked Ezra, watching Gabe's reaction to the stack.

"Yeah, and it looks to be ancient. I reckon it's markin' the trail. This'n," he pointed at a flat stone that was obtruding to the left side, "'pears to be pointin' down the trail, toward the confluence yonder. Seems to be pointin' a little to the east. Reckon it's to tell whoever that is the way to go! So," he stood up and looked down valley, "reckon that's what we'll do!"

"Uh, weren't that what we were already goin' to do?"

"Yeah, but . . ." he let the thought hang as he mounted the black, "It's always good to know we're goin' the right direction!"

"Now, what would a bunch of ancient travelers know about where we want to go?" asked Ezra as he nudged the bay to follow the grey packhorse behind Gabe.

"Oh, it's not so much about where we're goin' as it is the best way to be goin'," retorted Gabe over his shoulder.

They followed the ancient trail down the long draw that most often was sided by steep-shouldered buttes lined with rimrock on one side, long sloping shoulders on the other. The only vegetation was clumps of sage, greasewood, or rabbitbrush. Occasional clusters of buffalo grass and prickly pear and cholla cactus sprouted colorful blooms of yellow and pink. The meandering creek offered clusters of sego lily blooming white and shooting star showing bright purple. Chokecherry bushes were showing long whitish blooms, promising a bounty of fruit in mid-summer. Gabe pointed to a patch of bright purple blooming flowers at the edge of the hillside, "Keep your animals away from that, that's locoweed!"

"That's the stuff they like but drives 'em crazy?" asked Ezra.

"That's it. There's also some that blooms white, so avoid anything like it!"

With a glance at the sun that was struggling to show itself from behind the gathering clouds, Gabe nosed Ebony to cross the creek below the confluence and went to the shade of a tall creekside cliff. "Let's let 'em have a rest and get sumpin' to eat!"

"I'm all for that!" answered Ezra, as he stepped down and started loosening the girth.

Gabe removed the case with the telescope from his saddlebags and nodded toward the hilltop behind them to tell Ezra he was going for a look around. With a wave to Wolf, they started a zig-zag route to the pinnacle. Once at the point of rocks at the crest, he stretched out the scope and began his survey of the countryside. He spotted movement at the edge of the valley where a small creek joined the bigger stream. Several people were at the creekside, apparently digging for roots or something. With a lingering look at the group, he moved the scope to the hills and spotted the tips of four or five teepees. He guessed the distance to be about two miles, maybe a little less and, with the village nearby, those were probably just the women that were gathering plants and such. That would also mean the men were somewhere close, probably on a hunt or scout for animals.

As he continued his scan, he saw several riders coming towards the people near the stream and supposed them to be the returning men. He watched for a few moments longer and expanded his survey to include the high mountains behind and to the north. The black clouds were rolling across the high mountains and a sudden flash of lightning told of the storm. In the mountains, it is easy to see storms a great distance away, and this storm was heavy and broad. The sheets of water looked like long slanted grey lines extending from the clouds to the terrain below and the occasional jagged lances of lightning told of the fierceness of the storm. Gabe knew that kind of mountain cloudburst could bring torrents of water crashing down in flash floods that could drown unsuspecting animals and people. The first rumble of thunder rolled down from the black clouds and reverberated through the valleys and the foothills.

Gabe made a quick look at the people below them, the women gathering plants and such, then crabbed backwards off the crest to return to their temporary camp. He slipped and slid down the steep slope, often bouncing off his tail as he followed Wolf. The two scrambled into camp to confront Ezra as he sat leaning against the cliff face, hat over his eyes and arms folded across his chest. He pushed the hat back, saw Gabe's expression, "What's got you all stirred up?"

"Big storm comin'. It's coming from the high-up and pouring down more water'n these gullies can hold. We need to find shelter, but . . ." he frowned, shaking his head as he looked at his friend.

Ezra frowned, "I know that look! But what?"

"There's some folks downstream that will get swamped if they don't get away from the stream 'fore the floodwaters come."

"What folks?"

"Natives."

"What natives?"

"Dunno. They got a few teepees back up a draw that prob'ly won't get swamped but those women and kids sure will."

"How do you do it?" asked Ezra as he started tightening the girth on his saddle.

"What?"

"Out here, in the middle of nowhere, you still manage to find somebody that needs help. Somebody that we have to go rushing after and save, like some damsel in distress."

"Just a knack, I guess," laughed Gabe as he dug heels to Ebony.

They knew they could not go rushing up to the people, they would think they were being attacked, but there was little time to waste. Gabe hollered to Ezra, "Where they're diggin', they can't see how bad that storm is! They prob'ly know it's comin', but . . ."

Ezra glanced over his shoulder to see the high buttes and hills between them and the storm, with the only thing visible being the towering pillars of grey above the black-bottomed clouds. An occasional flare of light told of a bolt of lightning below and the rolling thunder gave notice of its movement but little else could be seen.

Gabe kicked Ebony to an easy canter and, within moments, they were approaching the plant gatherers. Two men sat horseback nearby and quickly moved toward Gabe and Ezra as they approached. Gabe reined up and waited for the two warriors, holding up one hand, palm open and facing forward, to indicate their peaceful intents.

Both warriors held weapons at the ready, one with an arrow nocked on his bow, the other with a lance at his shoulder. They moved their animals with leg pressure and the horses stopped when bidden. The one with the lance, lifted his chin to point at Gabe, "Who are you and why are you here?" he asked in the Shoshonean language, the tongue that was common to both the Shoshone and the Ute people.

"I am Spirit Bear. This," nodding to Ezra, "is Black Buffalo. We come in peace."

"Why are you here?" demanded the warrior.

"We came to warn your people of the coming storm."

The warrior frowned, glancing to the heavy clouds beyond the mountains. "You think we do not know of the storm?" he asked, incredulity showing in his expression.

"You cannot see the heavy rains it carries. We were there," stated Gabe, pointing to a high promontory, "and could see the heavy waters and we could see the women and children near the stream. If the floods come before they leave, they will not get away. They should return to your village now."

The warrior frowned, looking from Gabe and Ezra to the clouds, "I do not believe it to be so bad." He looked to his companion, then to the women. With a nod to his friend, the man went to warn the women. "They will go to their lodges." He glared at Gabe, "Why you do this?"

"We don't want to see your women and children drown. It is the right thing to do."

"I am Slow Turtle of the *Caputa* people. This is *Caputa* land. I ask again, why are you here?"

"We are bound for Santa Fe to get supplies. We live beyond the land of the *Tabeguache* and have wintered with the *Mouache.* We were told by Walkara of the *Tabeguache* we would find the *Caputa* people in this land and that we would find them friendly, as were the others."

The warrior frowned, looking from Gabe to Ezra, then noticed the big wolf belly down on the far side of the black horse. He looked back at Gabe and down at the wolf and started to speak when the second warrior rode up and shouted, "The women cannot find two of the children. They were hunting rabbits and wandered away!"

Gabe spoke up, "If they're not found before those floods come, they'll be washed away, sure!"

Slow Turtle was anything but slow as he reined his mount around to go look for the boys. Gabe motioned to Ezra, "Let's go!"

The impromptu search party began to comb the deep grasses and brush for two boys, both eager young hunters wanting to prove themselves. Gabe stood in his stirrups, searching the brush and more, until movement far from the stream near a thicket of rabbitbrush caught his eye. He tossed the lead to the packhorse to Ezra, slapped legs to Ebony and started toward the brush, hopeful of finding the boys. Wolf was at his side as they approached the thicket. He shouted in the tongue of the people, "Boys! Boys! There's flood coming!"

Suddenly, he spotted a black topknot and nudged Ebony closer. The two boys had bagged a rabbit and had it roasting over a small flame and were startled when the big black horse broke through the brush. One boy grabbed for his bow and Gabe shouted, "Do not touch your bow!" as he extended his hand toward the boy. Wolf stepped into view and lowered his head, growling. The boys moved closer to one another, staring wide-eyed at the big wolf, with only a glance to the white man.

"Your mothers are looking for you! The floodwaters are coming! Go!" shouted Gabe, pointing toward the creek and the others who were searching for them.

The boys turned and ran, without a backward glance, as they crashed through the brush and tall grasses. When they came to the creek, they splashed across, shouting, "*Shin-ab! Shin-ab!*" One woman grabbed a boy by the hand and jerked him around and started to the village at a run, dragging the boy behind. Slow Turtle stepped down from his horse beside the second boy, lifted him aboard the horse and swung up after him, and headed for the village.

Gabe chuckled, looked to Ezra who sat on his bay, holding the lead lines of both the grey and the mule as Ezra said, "Now what?"

Gabe shook his head, "We find shelter." He stood in his stirrups, twisted around, and pointed to the draw past the thicket of rabbitbrush where the boys had been, "I think I saw an overhang up that draw that might do the trick. C'mon." He reined Ebony around and with a glance toward the coming storm, clucked to the black as they started up the draw at a canter. Within less than a half-mile, they came to the overhang Gabe had spotted from the previous promontory when he scoped the countryside. It was deeper than expected and they rode up the slope and into the opening and quickly stepped down. They looked around, saw it was a site that had been often used, black covered the ceiling from previous campfires, wood was stacked against the wall, and a fire ring of stones invited their use.

Ezra filled the coffee pot with water from the stream below while Gabe started the fire. When Ezra returned, his hat and shoulders wet from the first bit of rain, he grinned and said, "Ain't this cozy! Nice place to wait out the storm!"

8 / SHELTER

The storm rolled on the crescendo of thunder, the monstrous claps bouncing off the canyon walls and hillsides. Lances of lightning added their cacophony of irregular rhythm as the forces of the Creator beat out their sounds of unrest. Gabe and Ezra stood under the overhang of the massive limestone, watching the torrent loose its fury as it marched across the foothills, sending the drumming rain to fill the gullies and arroyos. Every hillside, slope, and talus became a pathway for rainwater, the adobe soil shedding the downpour as the terrain shrugged its indifference. The water came at a slant, like the blades of ancient knights, flashing and driving and clearing everything in its path. Top-heavy trees strained at the shallow roots and toppled, diverting the rivulets to form new channels for the runoff.

A massive thunderclap shattered the stillness of

the shelter and bounced around the rock walls with a deafening roar. Lightning stabbed at the tall ponderosa that dared to lift its head above the juniper and piñon, splitting the rough-barked trunk and bringing sputtering flames that were quickly doused by the downpour. The raging wind howled like vengeful banshees, blowing the rain parallel to the ground, slamming it into anything that dared to stand in its way. And the storm marched on, parading through the valley, and strutting into the flatlands.

Close behind the rolling black clouds, another muted roar began to grow, announcing the coming of the floodwaters. Dirty white foam rolled before the angry waves that carried muddy water, splintered trees, entangled deadwood, and debris that included drowned animals, large and small. The small stream that guided the trail followed by Gabe and Ezra, converged with the bigger stream that came from the high mountains and each valley carried floodwaters that angrily clashed and fought the cliff face to crash around the bend for its run to the flatland. The creek bottom spanned the valley about five hundred yards wide and everything green was submerged under the flood. The roar of waters began to subside as the valley widened and the rate of descent lessened. What had been a scenic stretch of greenery, flowers blooming, grass greening, and more, had become an almost placid lake, brown with islands of dirty foam, cartwheeling tree trunks, rolling carcasses of animals.

The calm after the storm spread across the foothills, a shaft of sunlight giving permission for pause and relief. Gabe stepped from under the overhang and looked to the sky, the dark storm clouds moving south, giving way to the blue patches of sky, and increasing islands of sunlight. The sun was lowering in the west and' with his hands outstretched, he stacked fingers to guess, "Looks to be a couple hours of sunlight left but," nodding to the terrain below the overhang, "that mud won't do for travelin'."

"Nope. 'Bout all we can do is eat and sleep!" declared Ezra, grinning at his friend.

"Your two favorite things to do!"

"Yessiree bob, it is that, sure an' certain!"

Gabe chuckled as he turned back to the maw of the overhang and fetched some of the dry wood that had been stacked by some traveler before them. He stirred up the coals, lay out the fresh wood, and grabbed the coffee pot. As he hefted the pot, he shook his head, "I'll get some more water from our canteens. You get some meat and what have you for something to eat."

"Gotcha!" responded Ezra as he went to the packs.

They were finishing the meal when the squishing sound of approaching horses coming through the mud warned of the approach of visitors. Wolf came to his feet at the edge of the dry ground, looking below toward the mouth of the arroyo. Gabe stepped to his side, rifle in hand, as he looked to see two riders making their way toward the overhang. He recognized Slow Turtle but the woman with him was unfamiliar. Gabe raised his hand high, called out, *"Miqú Tugú-run-n."* Slow Turtle smiled and repeated the greeting of *Hello my friend.* Gabe motioned them into the open-mouthed cavern and invited them to step down. Slow Turtle did, offered to help the woman and said, "She is my woman, my wife. She is called Red Nose."

"Welcome Red Nose," offered Gabe as he poured the visitors cups of steaming coffee.

The woman frowned but accepted the cup and mimicked her husband as he drank. After a sip, she frowned and held the cup at her lap. Ezra noticed her reaction, picked up a bag of sugar and offered her some, dribbling it from his hand into the cup. He stirred it with a small tin spoon and handed the cup back, "Now try it," he suggested.

When she took a small sip, her frown turned into a broad smile and she took another longer sip, nodding to Ezra. "What is that?" she asked, nodding to the bag.

"Sugar. It's like honey, to make things sweet."

"I like sugar," she declared, taking another drink of the now sweetened coffee.

Slow Turtle smiled but squirmed a little as he watched his wife drink. Gabe noticed his uneasiness and said, "It is good that you visit with us but I think there is more to your visit than to drink coffee. Do you need something from us?"

"We came to let you know we are grateful for your warning of the storm and for finding the boys that had wandered away. The one boy is the brother of Red Nose and often goes off on his own. Their," nodding to Red Nose, "father and mother were killed when our people were attacked by the Navajo. The boy, Chiquito, has been with us and the brother of their father since that time."

"We were glad to help and we are pleased he was found and is safe."

"You said you were going to Santa Fe to get supplies. Have you been there before?"

"No, this is the first time, why?"

"We have talked of going to Santa Fe also. Our people go there for a trade fair in the time before snow comes but we have things to trade and would like to go also."

"So, you're thinking of going with us to Santa Fe?"

"If you would have us. It would just be me and my wife. We would have our own supplies and she is a good cook."

Gabe glanced to Ezra and caught his expression when he heard she was a good cook. Gabe grinned as he shook his head slightly, turned back to Slow Turtle and said, "It would be good to have someone with us that knows the trails. We will leave at first light."

Slow Turtle grinned, glanced at Red Nose and back to Gabe. He stood, extended his hand and the men clasped forearms.

As they watched the two leave their camp, Ezra turned to Gabe, "Well, it will be good to have somebody along to do the cookin' and to have them with us might make our travelin' through Ute country a little safer."

"That's what I was thinkin' too. And since he knows the trails and such, we might make better time."

There was just a hint of light when Gabe and Ezra rode from the overhang. The rimrock topped ridge that held their shelter stood between them and the thin grey line of early morning. When they came from the arroyo, they kept to the high ground on the ancient alluvial plain on the north side of the wide valley that carried the muddy stream, now moving within its usual banks but full to the edge. The remains of the storm waters were evident; the grasses were humbled and lying flat and parallel to the creek, every rift held storm debris, branches, sticks, logs, and carcasses. They watched as Slow Turtle and Red Nose crossed the swollen creek, two loaded packhorses tugging on long leads behind.

As they neared, Gabe gigged Ebony to start off at a walk, motioned Wolf ahead, and Slow Turtle came alongside. Ezra followed Gabe and Red Nose trailed Slow Turtle which put her beside Ezra and her curious glances made Ezra chuckle to himself. It was nothing new to him for others to be inquisitive, knowing most had never seen a black man, and he wondered how long it would be before she voiced her curiosity.

They had ridden but a few miles when Red Nose asked, “I have never seen a man like you. Why are you so dark and have hair like a buffalo?”

Ezra grinned, cocked one eyebrow up and asked her, “Why are you dark skinned and have long black hair?”

Red Nose frowned, “I am *Caputa* Ute! I am what the Creator made me!” she retorted indignantly.

Ezra chuckled, “I am what the creator made me!”

Red Nose frowned again, “But I have never seen anyone like you.”

“Where I come from, there are many like me but there are none like you.”

Red Nose frowned, looked ahead at the trail and Ezra could tell she was thinking about what he said as she turned to look at him again. “Your name is Black Buffalo?”

“That is what some have called me. But my father named me Ezra.”

“Ez – rah?” she repeated.

“Yes, Ezra.”

They rode in silence for a while until Red Nose asked, “Where is this place where there are many like you?"

Ezra grinned, pointed to the east, "A place very far to the east, beyond those mountains," nodding to the long range of Sangre de Cristo Mountains, "and more beyond those. Beyond the great river, many moons travel."

She frowned, then asked, "Do your people fight with others like you?"

"Not like the different people of the plains and mountains. Many of my people are slaves and have to work for others."

"Slaves?"

"Yes, like when your enemies attack your people and take captives and make them work in their villages for their people."

She thought a moment, "My mother was taken by the Navajo but her father took her back. But the Navajo came again and killed my mother and father. They are our enemies."

Ezra glanced at Red Nose and thought *No matter where we go, there are always those evil people that think it is all right to make others their slaves.* He shook his head at the thought, wondering if it would ever change. He took a deep breath that lifted his shoulders and looked around, marveling at the great creation of Almighty God and said a silent prayer that the God of all Creation would one day balance the scales of injustice that is rendered by man on man.

9 / VISITORS

"That looks like the backbone of the world," declared Ezra, nodding toward the pinnacles of the Sangre de Cristo mountain. "With all that snow still clinging to the peaks, kinda makes 'em look like bones."

Gabe glanced to his left across the wide flats to take a lingering look at the incredible mountain range, "Yeah, now that you mention it, it does look like a backbone." He chuckled at the apt description, "And that long blanket of black timber lays on those ridges and slopes like it's tryin' to keep the shoulders and flanks warm."

"Sure is purty!" added Ezra, "Even this flat country with all the sage and cactus has its own kinda purty, don't it?"

"It does that," answered Gabe, then frowning he narrowed his eyes and cocked his head to the side, turned to Slow Turtle, "Are those hot springs up there where the steam is rising?" pointing to a thin pillar of steam rising from behind a low mound.

"Yes. My people often come here to bathe in the hot water."

Gabe grinned, turning back to Ezra, "Hot springs!" pointing to the rolling hills and the wispy vapors rising.

"We stoppin'?"

"I reckon. We both could use a good bath!"

Since there was little brush and no trees, Gabe and Ezra hung back below the rise while Slow Turtle and Red Nose took the first dip in the hot springs pool. As soon as they returned, Gabe and Ezra made for the water; blankets, and soap ready and tiptoed into the hot springs and sat down in the shallow pool. With their buckskins and union suits still on, they soaped up to wash their duds, then stripped down and lathered up. As they stepped from the water, they were brought up short by the sight of several riders approaching. They hurriedly climbed back into their clothes, dancing from one foot to the other as they struggled with the wet duds. They had intended for them to dry out on the way but they did not expect to be caught in the buff. Their moccasins had escaped the scrubbing and they sat down to slip them on, glancing toward the approaching riders. Gabe jumped to his feet as he snatched up his rifle and stuffed his pistol in his belt.

He did his best to appear somber and stern but the laughter of the riders split his face in a grin as he shook his head in embarrassment. Several warriors were pointing and laughing, but the most embarrassing was the women as they snickered and giggled. Slow Turtle walked from behind the mound, Red Nose at his side, and with a glance to Gabe and Ezra, he joined in the laughter. Gabe glared at him, "Fine lookout you are!"

There were six couples and as many children in the small band of *Caputa* Ute, all known by Slow Turtle. They had come from another band that was close akin to their own. As they reined up and stepped down, the children were chattering but held in check by the women. Two men joined Slow Turtle and came toward Gabe and Ezra, grinning as they approached. One grey-haired man stepped forward, "I am Moara, leader of my people," he paused as he looked at Gabe and Ezra, then continued, "This is Sowiette, war leader of my people."

Gabe stood his rifle on its butt at his side, "I am Spirit Bear and this," motioning to Ezra, "is Black Buffalo. We are friends of the Ute people."

The leader frowned as he looked Gabe up and down, then turned to Ezra and did the same. "Why are you in our land?" he asked, looking at Ezra.

"We are going to Santa Fe for supplies, Slow Turtle and his woman are traveling with us," answered Ezra.

Slow Turtle stepped near, "These men are friends to the *Caputa.* They have helped our people and have been with the *Tabeguache* and *Mouache.*"

Moara looked from Turtle to Gabe and with a glance to Turtle to include him in the comment, "The *Jicarilla* have been raiding far to the north and the Navajo have taken many captives from the Pueblos. The time of greenup has always been a time these people have made many raids."

"I thought this land was the land of the *Caputa.* Do these others raid this far north?" inquired Gabe, frowning.

"They do not raid this far north but the Comanche do and the Kiowa and Arapaho have been known to come to this land when the buffalo come north."

Gabe nodded, understanding and, with a glance to Turtle and Ezra, he looked back to Moara, "We will be watchful and we are grateful for your warning." He paused, looking at the anxious group, "we will leave you to the hot springs. Your people are anxious to get in the water."

The chief nodded, turning back to his horse and the needed blanket and more for their time in the springs. Gabe and the others went to their horses and stepped aboard, nudging their mounts to the previously used trail, bound to the south. Slow Turtle suggested they hold to the trail that followed the flanks of the ridges on the western edge of the valley. Gabe guessed the valley between the foothills on the west and the flanks of the Sangre de Cristo Mountains on the east was about eighteen miles across. The flatlands of the valley were marked by patches of green where ground water and springs were abundant and the browns and greys of the dry land marked with sage, greasewood, and cacti.

It was just past mid-day after leaving Moara's band at the hot springs that they came to the rushing waters of the Rio Grande del Norte. Although the banks were lined with gnarly cottonwood and an abundance of willows and berry bushes, the river was not as imposing as Gabe had pictured. With memories of the Mississippi and Missouri, the Rio Grande was but a little brother, measuring about a hundred feet wide and no more than belly deep on the horses. They made the crossing and chose a shady site with ample grass for a brief rest for the animals. Gabe approached Turtle, "Is this the same river that goes to Santa Fe?"

"Yes, but it makes a wide bend," he motioned with his hand and arm to indicate an arching bend to the east, "and we will save a day or more if we do not follow the river."

Turtle went to the edge of the clearing and looked south across the dry land that flanked the smaller foothills, he looked over his shoulder to motion to Gabe and as Gabe joined him, he pointed to the southeast, "This is the land of the Navajo, Pueblo, and Apache."

"And those are the bands that are raiding?" asked Gabe.

"Yes."

Gabe thought a moment, then asked Turtle, "We thought about traveling at night, the moon's just waning from full and it's been a cloudless day. It might be a good idea with those bands doin' their raiding."

Turtle frowned, looked at Gabe, "You would travel at night?"

"Sure, why not?"

"Most do not because of the legends our people tell our children. There are legends about the puma, the porcupine, and the bear. But many are about the wolf and the coyote, legends that are told to make the children behave and obey their parents."

"Well, I'd be more concerned about the raiding parties than legends. Besides, we have a wolf of our own that travels with us and can warn us of any danger."

Turtle grinned, glancing at Wolf who stood beside Gabe, then nodded. "We can stay here until the sun goes to sleep, then we can ride."

"Then maybe we should be gettin' some firewood and maybe some fresh meat," suggested Gabe, turning to look at Ezra who was resting on the grass in the shade of a big cottonwood. He walked close by, spoke to Ezra, "How 'bout we go get some fresh meat? We're gonna wait till dark to travel further."

"You know, I was just thinkin' about how good

some fresh trout would taste." He frowned, glanced from Red Nose to Turtle, "You folks eat fish?"

"Yes, we eat fish, but they are hard to catch. It is easier to take a deer or antelope."

"Well, you go downstream, Spirit Bear will go upstream, and I'll go fishing. If you get a deer or such, fine, but I know I can get us some trout. I done seen some when we were crossing and it won't take long to get enough to feed us all," declared a grinning Ezra, hitching up his britches and going to the packs for his gear.

10 / SMOKE

The silver moon stood high above the black shadows of the Sangre de Cristo Mountains off the riders' left shoulders. The stars had lit their lanterns and taken their places with the Great Bear high overhead and the great Hunter near the moon. With the north star at their back, Gabe and company took to the trail, the dim blue glow of night accented by the alkali flats that strutted their white blanket that marked the west edge of their chosen trail. The foothills and the distant mountains bordered the nightscape with black silhouettes that showed the jagged horizon as an uncertain shadow.

Wolf trotted before them, head high and enjoying his realm, ignoring the lonesome wail of a coyote that went unanswered. The horses were rested and eagerly stepped out at a brisk pace in the coolness of the night. Cicadas filled the night with their racketing clatter, out of sync with the shuffling gait of the horses. Gabe and Ezra sided one another, comfortable in their oft-used manner of travel. Ezra looked to his friend, "Sometimes I wonder if you ain't part bat! The way you like to flitter around in the dark, just like 'em."

"I just like the quiet. With a moon like that one," nodding to the silvery orb, "we can see 'bout as much as we can in the daytime and the night blanket just quiets everything. It's comforting, somehow."

"That's prob'ly why most folks like to sleep at night, like we're s'posed to!"

The alkali flats gave way to grassy flatland, the change in temperature immediately evident. While the alkali and dry land retained the heat, the grassland absorbed it and made the temperature more moderate. The horses kept their pace, snatching mouthfuls of grass without missing a step, always alert for whatever the darkness might hold. Ezra commented, "One thing I never thought of 'bout travelin' at night."

"What's that?" asked Gabe, leaning forward on the pommel of the saddle, arms crossed as he looked sideways at his friend.

"Them rattlesnakes that like to sun themselves in the daytime, have gone to ground at night and ain't no bother at all!"

Gabe chuckled, "You're right about that. But the coyotes are more active and when they chase a jackrabbit out in front of your horse, he'll act just like it was a rattlesnake!"

Ezra laughed, "You're just sayin' that to keep me awake." He glanced to the moon, now hanging over the western mountains, looked back to the east, "What'chu figger, another couple hours 'fore daylight?"

Gabe did the same look around, "Yeah, 'bout that."

"We gonna make camp 'fore daylight?"

"Prob'ly."

Silence settled once again over the travelers, the steady rhythm of the shuffling gait, the creak of leather, and the clatter of hooves on the rocky trail offering a discordant lullaby to the weary travelers. Ezra's head was bobbing and Gabe was getting drowsy until Wolf stopped, dropped his head and caused Ebony and the bay to stop, heads up, ears forward, looking into the darkness of the trail before them.

Gabe sat up, moving side to side to try to pierce the darkness. He glanced at Ezra, "Smell that?"

"Yeah, smoke. But that ain't no campfire. That's burning flesh and more." The stench of burning flesh, once branded into a man's consciousness, is never forgotten nor mistaken. Ezra looked to Gabe, "What'chu thinkin'?" he whispered. He knew that somewhere before them, someone had died a terrible death, the kind of death that doesn't usually happen by accident. In that moment, memories, all of them unpleasant, filled their minds. The times when they had come upon villages that had been put to the torch and women and children had perished in the flames.

Gabe tossed the lead line for the grey packhorse to Ezra, "Wait here. I'm gonna take a look around." He nudged Ebony forward, Wolf stepping out ahead of them but moving stealthily as if on the prowl. Wolf paused, dropped his head and went into an attack stance, a low growl rumbled from his chest and Gabe slipped to the ground beside him. With his Ferguson in hand, Gabe moved in and out of the tall sage, the bitter scent contrasting with the stench of burning flesh. The gurgle of a stream came from further on, beyond some thick brush. Gabe was down on one knee beside Wolf, looking and searching the shadows of darkness. The only movement was a few embers climbing heavenward on the thin wisps of smoke that came from a smoldering pile of debris.

Unmoving, he searched the area by the dim light of the moon and could make out the remains of an adobe hut, the roof caved in and smoke rising from the framework. Beyond, where the embers still rose, a pile of burnt timbers crashed, stirring the coals in a brief flash of glowing cinders. Still nothing moved, Wolf dropped to his belly, no longer alarmed. Gabe rose to return to the others, moving in a low crouch, leading the big black.

"Looks like a farm; house, barn, all burnt. Prob'ly smellin' animals, maybe more. Can't tell till there's more light."

"So, it wasn't just an accidental fire," suggested Ezra, looking at his friend expectantly.

"No, not with the house an' barn far apart and both burnt. Reckon it was some o' them raidin' bunches the chief told us about."

Slow Turtle nodded, "Could be Navajo or Apache. Both raid against the Mexican farmers and villages."

"There's a river just past the farm. The breeze is comin' from the foothills to the west, yonder, so, how 'bout we move upstream a little, away from the smell and we can check it out come sunup," suggested Gabe as he stepped back aboard the big black. He called Wolf close and started toward the shadowy foothills to find a campsite near the river and away from the stench.

Yet no matter where they were, the stink seemed to follow.

As the thin line of early morning showed itself across the wide valley, Gabe nudged Ezra, "Let's go look," he stated, rifle in hand, as he slipped his neckerchief over his mouth and nose. Ezra stood, grabbed his Lancaster rifle from the scabbard and, as he started after Gabe, slipped his neckerchief over his mouth and nose, shaking his head as they headed into the stench.

They came to the remains of the barn, saw a partially burned carcass of a donkey and two goats that lay just outside the pole and brush corral, bloody but unburnt. The barn had been nothing more than a lean-to but was simply smoldering ashes now. Yet the reek was stronger as they neared the adobe walls that gaped with a sightless window and a black maw for a door. Gabe glanced at Ezra, shook his head, and stepped to the doorway. Two legs, mostly burned, protruded from under the burnt remains of the roof. He stepped inside, pushed the burnt end of a beam aside to see the burnt and swollen body of what was once a woman. He shook his head, put his hand to his neckerchief to hold it close to his nose, and turned away, picking his steps through the refuse to exit the structure.

Once free of the cabin, he stepped clear and jerked his mask down to gulp some fresh air. His thoughts were a mix of anger, revulsion, and pity. He glanced over his shoulder and thought of the couple that lay within, two people full of hopes and dreams, building a life together, and now everything gone. He shook his head knowing how often people just like this, in all walks of life, live as if they have all their tomorrows before them, time to make their dreams come true, and yet in nothing more than a day, have everything taken from them. He thought of his own family, hopeful they were safe, and he could soon return, and of his sister and her family back east. He walked away, looking around, trying to gulp whatever fresh air he could find and muttered a prayer of question to his God. "Why? These people probably never had a chance to know you God and now they never will. Why?" But there was no answer coming.

Ezra came near, "I've asked that question before and I remember my father quoting a scripture. It goes something like this, *For my thought are not your thoughts, neither are your ways my ways, saith the Lord. For as the heavens are higher than the earth, so are my ways higher than your ways, and my thoughts than your thoughts.* Then he'd tell me that even though we can't know what He's up to, we can have faith that it's always the best." He paused, rubbed the toe of his moccasin in the dirt then lifted his eyes to Gabe, "We don't know if they had a chance to know God or not but don't you think God would be more concerned about that than us?"

Gabe huffed, shook his head, "Yeah, prob'ly. It's just a good thing I ain't God!"

"Why do you say that?"

"Cuz if I was, I'd . . . I'd . . . I don't know what I'd do, prob'ly mess things up worse'n they already are!" He shook his head, chuckled, and looked at his friend.

Ezra chuckled, "So, what should we do?"

Gabe turned to look at his friend, shook his head,

"Not much we can do. If we tried to move them, we'd be picking up pieces for a week. I think we can just cave the walls in on them, make their home their grave."

Ezra looked at the small structure, three of the four walls still standing, "Yeah, I reckon you're right. I'm all for gettin' it done and movin' on across the river there, maybe find some place with fresh air."

11 / SIGN

Caving in the walls of the adobe hut was not an easy task, a job made all the more difficult by the worsening stench. The warmth of sunlight made the task doable but the rising stink from the heat of the day added to the challenges.

"I'll chip a hole through the clay, then we'll run the rawhide rope through, tie it around a chunk of wood and we can use the horses to pull it in on the pile," suggested Gabe, adding, "You get the rope and your horse ready; this won't take too long." They had already attempted to cave it in with pushing and kicking, ramming it with a piece of timber, but succeeded only in crumbling the top edge.

As Gabe and Ezra worked at the adobe walls, Slow Turtle carefully examined the sign around the area. He would often drop to one knee to touch and compare the sign, looking at both horse and man tracks. He was a careful man, always paying close attention to every detail. He noted the stitching on the edge of the moccasin tracks, the toed-in manner of walking, the numbers of different tracks. He stood and walked slowly toward the remains of the lean-to, and beyond, scanning the ground for all sign. With the recent heavy rain, it was easy to date the tracks, judging by the lay of the grass and weeds, the edge of each track, and any moisture in the soil. He followed the tracks to the edge of the river, stood on the bank and looked at the far side, and the disappearing trail of the raiding party.

The sudden rumble from the adobe hut brought Turtle's attention back to the rising dust and the men at work on the burial detail. He turned and walked toward Gabe and Ezra, glancing around at the evidence of the raid. The pile of burnt timbers still smoldered, a thin line of smoke rising slowly in a spiral, the donkey carcass was starting to bloat, and magpies and crows were already picking at the two goats by the fence.

Gabe and Ezra stood back looking at the pile of debris, dust and wispy charcoal still hung over the broken adobe bricks as Ezra looked at Gabe, "Think that's about the best it's gonna get!"

"I think you're right. And we prob'ly oughta be puttin' some miles behind us."

Slow Turtle stepped close, "There were ten or twelve raiders, Navajo. They took two horses and anything they," pointing with his chin to the make-shift grave, "had of value. They came before dark, went," nodding across the river, "into those hills. That leads to the land of the Navajo."

"Not Apache?" asked Gabe.

"No, Apache would bring woman out, use her and kill her. The man would be stripped and tortured to death." He pointed with his foot to a nearby moccasin track, "The moccasin of the Apache does not show stitching at the toe when they walk."

The track he pointed to raised Gabe's curiosity and he went to one knee for a closer look, reaching out to touch the distinct track. The shift of weight was evident by the roll of the foot, greater weight on the ball of the foot making a more distinctive impression, and the toe showed an indent with a line of stitching at the tip of the track. "That's the stitching there," stated Gabe as he pointed with his finger almost touching the track, "and the Apache moccasin does not have that?" he asked as he turned back to look at Turtle.

Turtle bent his knee, lifted his foot across his leg and pointed at his moccasin, "This stitching is like that, like the Navajo. But the Apache use the hide of a buffalo for the bottom and roll the hide over the toe. When they run, they stay on this part of the foot," cupping his hand over the ball of his foot, "and the toe is protected by the roll. The Apache go afoot as often as they ride and need the heavy bottom and toe covering."

He nodded downstream toward the greener bottomed flats, "The Apache would come from there and go back there." He turned and nodded to the confluence of the river and a smaller stream that came from the southeast, "The raiders, Navajo, went that way."

"So, what you're sayin' is, we're going to Apache country?" asked Ezra.

"Santa Fe is in the land of the Pueblo or Tewa people and the *Jicarilla* Apache."

Ezra frowned, looked at Gabe, "Did you know that?"

"No but wherever we go, somebody has been there before us. In this case, it's the Tewa and Apache. Why should it be any different?" Ezra shook his head, mumbling as he turned away, leading his big bay back to the camp where Red Nose waited with the packhorses. Gabe chuckled and followed.

The ancient trail chosen by Turtle bound southeast across the dry land flat. They were determined to put some miles behind them, even though it meant traveling in daylight. The sun bore down as the dust lifted with every footfall. The muffled steps of the horses became more of a shuffle, the heat bringing sweat and lather beneath the gear, heads hanging and nostrils flaring. Gabe motioned for a stop, stepped down, and started walking, leading the tired horses, even though the dust whirled around their feet at every step. The heat was stifling and sweat dribbled down their back and chest while, at their neck, the sweat mixed with dust and made mud balls. Within about fifteen miles, the dry land with its brittle grasses and cacti finally gave way to green. The bunchgrass, grama, and Indian grasses showed green, rabbitbrush blooming yellow took the place of purple-tinted sage and grey greasewood. The riders stepped back aboard horses that lifted their heads, pricked their ears and flared their nostrils at the promise of water. The green leaves of rugged cottonwoods contrasted with the fluttering thin leaves of willows and alders but all promised water. The horses quickened their pace and the entourage soon came to the bank of a small river, no more than twenty-five feet across, but flowing with clear, cold, water. Riders dropped to their bellies beside the noses of the horses and everyone eagerly absorbed as much of the refreshing water as possible.

Gabe led Ebony into the water, standing beside him as they both cooled their heels, knee deep in the gurgling stream. Ebony dipped his nose in, sloshed around and splashed water on Gabe, but there was no complaint from the dusty rider. The grey packhorse had been following rein-free and had followed Ebony into the water. He put his face in the water, blew some bubbles, and lifted his head to shake the water from his mane and face.

Ezra had followed Gabe into the water and sat down, the stream coming to his shoulders. The cold water was stimulating and he laughed all the while. "Whooeee! After that hot springs bath and that trek across those alkali flats, this shore do feel good!"

Slow Turtle and Red Nose stood side by side on the bank, watching the antics of their two new friends. Red Nose smiled and giggled, Turtle just shook his head, grinning. Gabe looked at the two, "Might as well come in, it does feel good!"

"We will bathe after we make camp," stated Turtle, turning away from the stream.

Red Nose had prepared a fine meal of fresh venison steaks roasted over the fire, cattail roots and osha roots roasted in the coals, and cornbread made with the help of Ezra. The men were sitting back and enjoying the remaining bit of coffee when Ezra said, "You know, all the while we were riding after leaving that farm, I wondered what in the world were those people doing there? In all our explorations and such, that was the first settler we found anywhere near the mountains!" he declared.

"I was wondering the same thing," replied Gabe. He looked to Turtle, "Are there many settlers between here and Santa Fe?"

Turtle looked back at Gabe, then to the ground, thinking. He raised his eyes to Gabe and Ezra, "He is the first to be so far into the country of my people. Where we go, there are many pueblos, villages of the Tewa people. They are a people that stay in one place, raise their food in the fields, have their own animals, hunt little. They have been there since before their grandfather's grandfathers. They have few enemies for their houses of mud are strong and great. But the others, like those in Santa Fe, what many call Mexicans, go to many places and build little lodges and have animals and raise plants in the fields. They go where there are no others, then others come. The people you buried had not been there long. They thought they would be safe away from the Apache but still they died because they came into a land that was not theirs."

Gabe thought about it a bit, glanced at Ezra who was also staring at nothing yet considering what Turtle said, then with a glance to Turtle, Gabe said, "One day, there will be people like us," pointing to himself and Ezra, "that will come into your lands and try to raise crops in fields and animals to eat. That seems to be the way of people, always looking for more."

"Why do they not stay where they are? Is it not a good place?" asked Turtle.

Gabe grinned, slowly shook his head, "Yes, but people that have little, want more. And there are always more people coming." He paused, trying to word his thoughts so Turtle could more easily understand. "Where we came from, the people want to own property. To have a place to build their lodge, make a home, have a family. Back there," pointing to the east, "there are too many people for everyone to go hunting for food and they have to grow it or raise it and that takes room and land. And if they don't have enough, they leave there, come west, and take more."

"Man cannot own land. It is the Creator's, not ours. We can use it, hunt for our meat, dig for our roots and things, then move on and let things grow again. When we come back, there will be more and we can have our family and our lodge. What you say about your people is not good. They do not know these things?"

"At one time they did, but now . . ." he shook his head in wonder and consternation, knowing it was difficult for Turtle to understand. Gabe knew the people and he did not always understand, not after seeing the vastness of the west and the simple life of the denizens of the wilderness. It made Gabe a little sad to think about what would probably happen if this land ever became open to settlers, the way they would change everything and everyone that now made this part of God's creation so wonderful. But such is the way of people, at least the people of the east who had little respect for the land and the natives that live here. He sighed heavily, looked at the sun that was past mid-day and suggested, "Maybe we all better try to get some sleep before we start out again after dark. It's already been a long day."

12 / FLATS

Gabe and Turtle rode side by side, the halfmoon hanging brightly over their left shoulders. The clear sky was littered with stars and bedecked with the wide band of the milky way. Coyotes howled their melancholy chorus, nighthawks let their cry fill the night air, and Wolf padded silently before them on the trail of the ancients. In the distance, the round dome of a shadowy mountain appeared out of place in the midst of the flatlands. Gabe had sighted it from their camp by the river and guessed it to be a long-dormant volcano. When they neared the mound, Turtle said, "Bear Mountain," as he pointed with his chin to the tree-covered monolith that stood a half-mile above them. Gabe saw the massive clumps of basalt, crowded by ponderosa and scrub oak, noticed the split top of the butte and knew his observation that it was an ancient volcano was accurate.

Turtle added, "Plenty game. Elk, deer, pronghorn, rabbit."

In the moonlight, the lower shoulders appeared as dark stripes of finger ridges bearing the black timber and bald ridges but the upper reaches of the mountains bristled with vast aspen groves covering most of the northern summit and slopes. It was an anomaly, standing as a lone sentinel in the expansive flats that stretched for miles in every direction. Yet, in the distance were two or three smaller mounds that rose about eight miles away. Without these few blemishes to the flats, there would be no landmarks to measure distance, nothing to mark progress. And on they traveled.

Bearing due south, keeping the north star at their backs, the travelers made good time across the flats. The cool night air kept the horses and riders awake and alert, enjoying the serenade from the cicadas and the frogs from the nearby stream. The trail had split the tall volcanic mountain and the three lower buttes, sided the river a short distance, then bore a little southwest, drawing nearer the rolling timbered foothills. A few miles to the west, they came to a fertile but narrow valley, bottomed by a shallow meandering river. Turtle pointed to the south, "The trail follows the river to the long mesa. We will camp there before going beyond the mesa to the Rio Bravo."

Gabe reckoned they had made over thirty miles

and both horses and riders were tired and eager for a stop. Turtle led them to cross the shallow stream that lay in the shadows of the long mesa. The chosen trail of the ancients continued to the southwest as it rode the flanks of the tall mesa. Even in the dim light of early morning, the sparse piñons, juniper, and twisted cedar blanketed the steep slopes that rose to the long flat top. When Turtle saw Gabe leaning to the side to look up to the rimrock edge, he said, "The top of that mesa is barren, dry, and looks the same on the other side. It is long and is between these rivers," motioning to the two recently joined streams and another that came from the western mountains and converged near the point of the mesa, "and the Rio Bravo, what the Mexicans call the Rio Grande del Norte."

Turtle motioned to a thicket of cottonwoods, "We will stop there, good cover, water and grass."

The men stripped the horses, rubbed them down with handfuls of buffalo grass, and let them graze on the greenery at streamside. Gabe gathered the firewood, Ezra started the fire and prepared the coffee, and Red Nose busied herself with the food preparation. Gabe sat opposite Slow Turtle, glanced up and asked, "I've been wonderin', why were you the only one that wanted to go to Santa Fe for trading?"

"It is the time of *Mack-on-see-pi,* the Bear Dance. Many bands come together and have the ceremony of ridding themselves of the bad things, memories, and problems. Many sing new songs given by the spirits and most carry plumes of feathers that are left behind to show the leaving of bad things behind. It is a special time for all and many young people find their mates at the dance." He paused, smiling at some special memory of previous Bear Dances, then added, "But I am a man of *När-är-wop,* a trader of things for the people. I get supplies that many want and travel to other bands and make trade. Now I take those things," motioning to the packs carried by the horses, "to trade to the people at Santa Fe."

"Fascinating!" declared Gabe, glancing to Ezra and back to Turtle. "You are the first trader I've met among all the tribes we visited. Are there many that do as you do? Travel between bands, I mean."

Turtle grinned, "Among the *núuchi-u,* the people, there are many bands and many men of different skills that travel between the bands. Some are flintknappers and arrow makers, some are medicine men, some are tellers of stories, the stories of our grandfathers and more. We travel from band to band, for the *núuchi-u* are many people."

The sun was bending its rays over the crest of the mesa when the small group of travelers took to their blankets in the shade of the cottonwoods. The gurgling stream nearby served as the lullaby to lure the weary travelers to sleep. Wolf lay beside Gabe, the horses tethered close to the water and the narrow patch of grass on the creek banks. As Gabe rolled to his side, he was confident in the watchfulness of both Wolf and Ebony and was determined to get in at least a few hours of much-needed rest. But it was the distant sound of gunfire that brought him instantly awake. Wolf was on his feet, looking downstream of the small creek, the horses were standing, necks bent to look into the trees, ears pricked and nostrils flaring.

A quick glance to the sky told Gabe it was already mid-day although it seemed like minutes since he took to his blankets. He stood, rifle in hand, listening and watching. More intermittent gunfire, but obviously far away, rattled through the narrow draw, bouncing off the steep slopes of the bordering mesa. Ezra's voice came from behind him, "What do you make of it?"

"Dunno, somethin's happenin' but it's quite a ways downstream." He turned to look at Ezra and Slow Turtle, standing side by side, "You two stay here. I'm takin' my scope and headin' up that knob yonder. Maybe I can make out what's happening."

With Wolf at his side, Gabe dug his toes in the loose soil, reaching out with his hand for balance, and pushed his way to the top of the knoll. Quickly bellying down, he slipped the telescope from its case and stretched it out in the direction of the gunfire. About two miles downstream of the little creek, a displaced ridge and butte stood beside the cottonwoods and alders that sided the creek. From behind the butte rose grey and black smoke. Gabe carefully searched the area of the butte, saw several riders coming from the flats toward the back side of the rise, heard two more rifle shots, and then nothing. No riders, no gunfire, but the smoke continued to lift into the clear sky. He waited, watching, several minutes passing, until several riders and, judging by their attire or lack of it, they were obviously Indian, rode from the backside of the butte and rode toward the cut at the point of the long mesa. A handful of the riders were driving a bunch of riderless horses, others led horses with packs aboard. They disappeared around the point and Gabe again searched the area of the smoke but saw no more movement.

Gabe rose, slipped the scope into its case and with Wolf at his side, started back to the camp. As he walked into the clearing, Ezra and Turtle looked at him with expectant expressions, and he spoke, "Looks like some kind of raid. I couldn't see what was beyond a little knoll and ridge but it was next to the creek. Several riders left with a bunch of horses and heavy loaded packhorses. They were native but from this distance, I couldn't tell who they were, but they left the place burning."

"Where did they go?" asked Turtle, scowling.

"Through that cut to the south where you said we were going."

"Apache!" spat Turtle, his eyes flaring, nose wrinkling as he slowly shook his head in disgust.

Gabe was surprised to see Turtle's reaction and asked, "I take it you are not friends with the Apache?"

"The Apache are the enemy of all peoples! They can be friends one day, enemy the next. You cannot trust Apache!" he spat the words showing his contempt of the people.

Ezra looked at Gabe, "Does this mean we're goin' to see whatever the smoke is about?"

Gabe nodded, turning away, and going to the stack of gear. He brought Ebony close and began saddling the big black, "Sorry boy, I know you would have liked a longer rest but maybe we won't go so far." It was but a short while until all were saddled and ready, packhorses loaded, and stretched out on braided rawhide leads, and they took to the trail that pointed directly toward the rising smoke.

13 / HACIENDA

"Well, I never expected to see something like that!" declared Gabe as he reined up and sat on the slight rise looking down on the smoldering remains of a structure. He shook his head as he looked at what appeared to have been a Spanish Hacienda. A low adobe wall surrounded the U-shaped structure, giving a sprawling courtyard before the main building. The archway entrance had two massive gates that hung askew, the building's roof had caved in and smoldered, the clay tiles smothering whatever fire had destroyed the interior. A long veranda, mostly tumbled over, had several arches between the porch posts, but the adobe walls still stood, shuttered windows smashed in, and several bodies lay strewn about. Men who had been workers, apparently still building on the structure, wore the typical off-white britches and shirts, bandanas and sombreros, but now lay bloodied and burnt.

Gabe nudged Ebony forward, picking his way down the slight rise to cross the creek. The far bank rose steeply from water's edge but the wide flat bore ample grasses. Gabe noticed a large barn-type outbuilding that sat at the edge of a big pole corral but the gate lay against the fencing and the corrals sat empty. The ample sign showed this was where the horses had been kept but the raiders had taken every horse and left a pair of dead donkeys. Gabe shook his head as he neared the arched gateway, rode into the courtyard, careful to avoid the strewn bodies. Ezra and Turtle followed Gabe and all three stepped down to tether their mounts at the hitch rail that stood before the hacienda. Gabe looked at Ezra and Turtle, "You two check around outside here, look for any sign of life and I'll check the house. Take Wolf with you."

The two men nodded and turned to their task as Gabe looked at the door that stood ajar and stepped through the doorway. The burnt roof timbers had caved under the weight of the clay tile and covered most of the interior of the house. Near the walls, Gabe bent and twisted through the debris, looking for any occupants that may still be alive. He picked his steps carefully, smoke and dust filling his nostrils and everything he touched shed its black ash. He saw another doorway with the burnt door askew, stepped toward it and heard a low moan. He paused, listening and moved through the doorway. A big four-poster, canopied bed, the posts the size of his legs, sat near the window, the ceiling and roofing piled at the side where the canopy and posts had shed the debris as it fell. What used to be a woman, was sprawled on the bed, bloodied, and disfigured, scalped and mutilated, sightless eyes staring at the canopy. Gabe reached for a woven blanket to cover the body but another moan came from the far side of the bed.

Gabe cautiously moved around the end of the bed to see the form of a man, attired in the typical rig of a Spaniard nobleman, tailored and decorated britches, short coat that matched, but all was bloody. He lay face down, his back bloodied from more than one wound, and Gabe bent to roll him to his back. The man moaned; eyes fluttered in fear until he saw Gabe's face. He relaxed and asked, "My daughters, are they . . .?"

"I haven't found your daughters yet, but we are looking."

As he struggled to speak, the father choked on blood, spat a mouthful to the side, "Apache! No warning, . . ." he coughed, spat, "I had no men to fight. These were . . . laborers." He reached out, grabbing a handful of Gabe's tunic, "Save them! My daughters! . . . *por favor, te lo ruego!*" He choked, bubbles of blood coming at his lips, and fell back, dead.

Gabe looked at the man, turned to look at the remains of the woman, and felt bile rising in his throat.

He choked it down, smelling blood, death, ashes and more, and rose to his feet. He stumbled out of the crumbled home, stood on the porch leaning against a post and sucked air, forcing the bile to retreat. He spat, lifted his head, and looked around to see Ezra coming from behind the house, shaking his head and mumbling. Gabe frowned as Ezra drew near, looked at his friend and growled, "They're dead! Used and mutilated! Maybe fifteen years old, looks like they were twins!" he snarled as he shook his head in anger. He glanced to Gabe again, "If I catch the ones who did this . . . they will wish the avenging angels of God almighty had caught them first!"

Slow Turtle walked slowly around the far side of the house, coming toward Gabe and Ezra. He kept his head down, appearing unconcerned about the many dead that littered the courtyard, yet as he approached Gabe, he spoke without lifting his head. "Do not move. We are watched. On the ridge of the hill across the stream, two Apache."

Gabe casually looked at the ridge, saw two men, horseback, and sitting in open view atop the ridge, watching the hacienda.

"They watch to see what we will do. If we do not leave, they will signal the others to return. We are few, they are many. We have horses and a woman and weapons."

"How many?"

"There were at least twenty warriors."

"Yeah, that's 'bout what I figgered when I saw 'em leave earlier." He looked back to Turtle, "You think they would come back?"

"We are four, they would send back two hands or more. The others would keep their bounty from the early fight and return to their rancheria."

"But you said we would be going the same way they went, so, where do we go?"

"Let's go from here, then decide," suggested Turtle. "But do not look like we are running away."

Gabe looked from Turtle to Ezra, nodded and started for Ebony. With a wave of his hand, he kept Wolf close by and started toward the archway entrance to the courtyard. Red Nose waited beyond the walls with the packhorses and without pause, Gabe reached out for the lead to the grey and kept moving, Ezra doing the same. Turtle spoke from behind, "When this stream joins the river, cross the river. The Apache stayed on this side, to have the river between us is best."

Gabe nodded, gigged Ebony to a trot and glanced across the creek to see if the Apache still watched, but they were gone. Another glance to the left showed a dust trail where the two lookouts were chasing after the rest of the raiders, probably to give their report. Gabe looked over his shoulder, "Let's pick up the pace! They've gone for the others!" He slapped legs to the big black and Ebony lunged forward, Gabe tightened his grip on the lead of the packhorse and leaned forward, giving Ebony his head.

It was less than a mile to the confluence of the creek and the Rio Chama. The muddy river was about a hundred feet wide but a quick look showed a crossing just downstream from a sand bar island that slowed the current of the shallow river. Without hesitation, Gabe pushed Ebony to the water and the big stallion eagerly waded into the muddy stream. As they crossed, the water failed to reach Ebony's belly and the gravelly riverbed gave good footing. When the others came from the water, Gabe nudged Ebony on, even though the big black tried to shake the water free, he responded to his rider's urging and stepped out in the lead.

A stretch of the bank was almost bare of the usual cottonwood and offered a view of the east side and the trail taken by the Apache. The big mesa that had shadowed the small creek and their previous campsite ended in an abrupt point at the east bank of the Rio Chama but the flank of the mesa provided a well-used trail and a rising shoulder that held a higher trail. It was on the high trail that Gabe caught sight of the two lookouts making their way toward the other raiders. They had slowed their pace and Gabe reined up to look further on the hillside trail. The long slope from the stream to the mesa top was sparsely covered with piñon and juniper but a small cluster of juniper showed several horses standing in the shade of the broad trees.

He nodded toward the group, "That's the rest of the raiders, there, by that clump of juniper." He guessed the shoulder of the slope where the raiders waited was about three hundred fifty, maybe four hundred yards from the near bank.

"What do you suppose they're up to?" asked Ezra, looking from the raiders to Gabe.

"I reckon that's gonna depend on what the lookouts tell 'em."

Ezra stood in his stirrups, looking at the nearby terrain, "The only thing we got goin' for us is the river between us. But they got us outnumbered by a whole bunch!"

"Ummhmm," answered Gabe, also looking around. "C'mon," he added, nudging Ebony downstream, keeping the cottonwoods, alders, and scrub oak as cover for their movements. He rode far enough to be at a point directly across the river from the raiders that still stood on the shoulder of the slope as they watched their lookouts come near.

Gabe pulled Ebony to a stop behind a thicket of cottonwoods, stepped down and slipped the case with his Mongol bow from beneath the left stirrup fender. As Ezra stepped down, Gabe went to a nearby log and removed the bow from its case, lay the case beside the quiver of arrows, and asked Ezra, "Pick me out a good 'un," nodding at the arrows.

Gabe put his feet, one on either side of the grip and reached for the limbs to string the bow. With considerable effort, he bent back the laminated limbs, slipped the waxed and woven string over the nocks, and released the limbs. He stood, bow in hand, and slipped the jade thumb ring over his thumb and started for the trees. Ezra slipped his rifle from the scabbard and followed Gabe, checking his load as he moved. Gabe went closer to the river's edge, found a stretch without heavy trees and brush, and stepped into the open, looking at the raiders on the far slope.

He watched as the group drew near the returning lookouts as they slid to the ground from their horses. As they stood before the others, one man stepped closer, obviously the leader, and Gabe took aim. With his fingers wrapped around his thumb in a fist, the thumb ring on the bowstring, he stepped into the bow with the one-hundred-pound draw weight and brought it to full draw. He lifted the bow, nocked arrow in place and sighted down the shaft, lifted the bow slightly higher for the distance, and let the arrow fly. It whispered high overhead, arched, and started plummeting to the ground. The shaft struck the ground between the leader and the lookouts, startling everyone that saw it strike. The leader jumped back, dropped into a crouch, and looked in the direction of origin of the arrow. He saw nothing but the whisper of another made him lift his eyes. That arrow drove itself into the man's thigh, driving him to his back as he screamed his surprise and shock.

The other warriors dropped to the ground, searching for the shooter, but they, like most would, limited their search to the area of brush below them and on the near bank of the river. Then they heard a shout, looked to see two men standing on the far side. The Apache looked at one another and at the men on the river bank until another shout came in the tongue of the Ute. Gabe had cupped his hands at his mouth and shouted as loud as possible, "I am Spirit Bear; this is Black Buffalo. You killers of women and helpless! You follow, you die!" The words echoed across the narrow canyon, bouncing off the talus slope and back again.

The warriors looked from one to another until one man spoke, "He speaks the tongue of the Ute. They are Spirit Bear and Black Buffalo. He said we are killers of women and helpless ones. If we follow, we die."

The others came to their feet, shouting and screaming their war cries until they heard a high-pitched screaming whistle coming toward them. Gabe had chosen a whistler arrow to make his point and it arched high, began to drop toward them, but the men were stunned by what they heard and were frozen in place until the arrow drove into the chest of the nearest warrior, making him stumble back and fall. The arrow had pierced his bone hairpipe breastplate, driving completely through, leaving only the fletching exposed at his chest. The warriors were stunned, looked at their fallen friend, and stepped back to look at the two men on the far side of the river. The warriors looked at one another, chattering and pointing, and stepped away from the edge of the shoulder, refusing to expose themselves further.

When Gabe saw the warriors drop down and away from the edge of the shoulder, he turned to Ezra, saw Turtle standing agape beside him and said, "Let's git, while the gittin's good!" and trotted to the trees. The others followed him and they quickly mounted, Gabe in the lead, and took to the trail, kicking the horses to a canter to put some miles behind them.

14 / VILLAGE

The black stallion stretched out, the grey packhorse keeping pace showing slack in the lead rope. Gabe leaned into the flying mane. Ebony loved to run and Wolf ran with him. The trail shadowed the river as it wound its way through the valley bottom, cottonwoods, alders, willows, oak, all riding the river banks, deep roots hoarding the moisture that would be in short supply with the coming of the summer heat. The ancient dusty trail was an easy trail and within a short while, the small group had traversed a couple miles prompting Gabe to slow the pace. As he pulled Ebony back to a walk, Turtle came alongside, "We are near the village *La Vega de los Vigiles.* They have always been at peace with the Apache and we will be safe there."

"Very big village?" asked Gabe.

"There are many lodges," replied Turtle. "We,"

motioning to Red Nose, "will go on to the Pueblo, trade with the Tewa."

"Will we meet you at this Pueblo?"

"The Tewa are not friendly to you," pointing to Gabe with his chin, "they only meet people they know. I have traded with them before."

They walked the horses for a spell until Gabe spotted a dust cloud indicating several riders on the far side of the river and well behind them. With another nudge to the big stallion, the horses stretched out again, covering a couple more miles before slowing. Gabe reined up, stepped down, "Let's walk 'em a little, let 'em catch their wind," he announced to the others as he searched the far bank for any sign of pursuers but there was none.

The sun was dropping behind the western hills when they rode into the village. Most of the buildings were flat-topped adobe, small windows, and single doors. A few signs hung over the doors of any business, yet there was nothing to distinguish the businesses from the residences. A corral with two horses and a hay mow, a lean-to with a blacksmith forge and anvil, had a gate with a swinging sign, *Estable.* Gabe swung down and approached the man at the anvil, spoke in Spanish, "Can we stable our horses and gear?"

"Si, si. Dos pesos."

Gabe frowned, "Two pesos per horse?"

"No, no. Dos pesos, all horses," responded the paunchy, mustachioed smitty, grinning broadly and showing brown teeth, what there were of them.

"Is there a place to eat, maybe get a room for the night?"

The smitty looked at Gabe, then frowned as he saw Ezra, and raised an eyebrow when he looked at Turtle and Red Nose. He looked back at Gabe, "They will not take Indians," he growled.

Gabe chuckled, "Our friends will not be staying. They are going to the Pueblo."

The smitty relaxed, nodded his head and motioned down the dirt street, "The Cantina Morales has good food, a few rooms but they're not much." He started to turn away, then added, "If you're stayin', turn your horses in the corral. You can stack your gear there," pointing to a corner of the lean-to with his pincers.

Gabe reached in his pocket, brought out two silver dollar coins, handed them to the smitty, "That's a little more than two pesos but take care of our gear and keep it." The smitty grinned, nodding, and after a quick examination of the coins, abruptly jammed them into his pants pocket beneath his leather apron.

Slow Turtle looked at Gabe, "The pueblo is not far. We will see you and if we go to Santa Fe with you, we will come with you. We might stay with the Tewa."

Gabe reached up to Turtle, clasped wrists with the man, "It has been good to travel with you Turtle. If we do not see you again, may the Creator be kind to you."

"And to you, my friend," replied Turtle.

Gabe and Ezra watched the two start through the village, then turned to strip the horses of the gear. "Did that fella say there was a good place to eat near?" asked Ezra.

"He did. But he said the rooms weren't much."

"That's all right. Food's most important. We can sleep anywhere!"

"Yeah, but I'm not too anxious to meet up with the Apache again."

"I'd rather meet 'em with a full belly. *If* we have to meet 'em that is."

Gabe chuckled, stacked the gear in the corner of the lean-to and joined Ezra as they started down the dirt street toward the cantina. It was little different from the other adobe structures, the sign was faded and barely legible, but the door opened as a man stepped through the doorway and the delightful aroma of spicy food invited the two inside.

A portly woman with a colorful long skirt, a white flared waist blouse, and a flowery apron greeted the two, "Welcome, welcome! Have a seat, señors!" waving at an empty table. Gabe was surprised the woman spoke in English and answered, "Thank you," and took the offered seats at the table. She came to their side, rested her hand on Gabe's shoulder, smiling at both men and said, "And what is your pleasure, señors?"

"We'd like something to eat. Been on the trail a while and we're a mite hungry," answered Gabe.

"That's what I like to hear. Do you want something special, or will you trust Mama Morales?"

Ezra chimed in, "We'll eat whatever you bring us, Mamacita!"

She smiled at Ezra, patted him on the shoulder and turned to the kitchen. Within moments, she returned with two platters of food, hot and steaming, and sat one in front of each of the men. "We have huevos with machaca, arrachera and cabrito with onions, potatoes, and chiles. And we have tortillas! Enjoy!"

And they did enjoy the unusual feast, washing it all down with champurrado, and sitting back with full stomachs. Mama Morales came back for the dishes, smiling, and asked, "Will you be with us long?"

"No, Mama, we're on our way to Santa Fe. But do you mind if we ask you a little about the area and such?"

She smiled, pulled out the extra chair and sat down, folding her hands across her ample middle as she looked from one to the other. "What can I tell you?"

"We ran into some unfriendly Apache upriver a little ways. What can you tell me about them?" asked Gabe, leaning forward.

"Ah, the Apache! They are a different people." She paused, then continued, "The Apache near here are the Jicarilla. They will be at peace with one village but not the next. They have been at peace with our village for some time. They come in and trade for supplies and are friendly. But they have no such peace with Santa Fe. They are at peace with the Tewa at the Santa Clara Pueblo but not with other pueblos. And that could change in a day. They could come into this town and want to kill everybody, no warning, no reason. So, we are always careful, always have our weapons near." She nodded to the door into the kitchen and the butt of a rifle was visible at the corner.

"There are two bands of the Apache. Northeast from here are the *Olleros,* the mountain people. They are friendly with the Caputa Ute. West are the *Llaneros,* or plains people. They are friendly with the Mouache Ute."

Gabe frowned, "Did you say the *Olleros* band of the Apache are friends with the Caputa Ute?"

"Yes. They have fought together against the Navajo and they trade together."

Gabe looked from the woman to Ezra, shook his head slightly, and added, "We came across a hacienda earlier today that the Apache had raided. Killed everyone and burnt the place. We had to leave before we could bury them because the Apache were watching us. That's what brought us here."

Mama frowned, "A hacienda? Where?"

"Upstream of a small creek the other side of the mesa, just before the confluence with the Rio Chama.

It *was* a nice place, but not now."

"That would be the Escalante hacienda. A fine family. They were building that hacienda and were going to expand their ranch. They had beautiful twin daughters." The words had come softly, reverently, and respectfully as only a true friend could show. She leaned back, looking from Gabe to Ezra, "Were you there when it happened?"

"No, we came upon it later. We heard the gunfire from the defenders but were too far away to help."

"And you say the Apache saw you?"

"Yes. Later."

"They will be after you. Be careful when you leave. They will be watching for you."

Mama rose, nodded to the men, accepted the coin from Gabe and went to the kitchen. They heard her speaking to some man who spoke angrily to her, then he came to the doorway and looked into the dining area, glared at Gabe and Ezra and turned back to the kitchen. There were more heated words exchanged but Gabe and Ezra had already risen and were going to the door. They stepped outside, dusk was settling over the land, and they looked around, seeing a few windows and doorways where lanterns had been lit but also noticed several doors closing and windows being shuttered. Gabe frowned, wondering, until they passed an open door, heard someone shout and a woman looked out, saw Gabe and Ezra and her eyes flared, her hand went to her mouth and she quickly shut the door. The window was shuttered and as they neared the lean-to, they glanced back at the now darkened street, then to one another.

Ezra said, "What is that all about? You'd think we were rattlesnakes or sumpin'!"

The smitty watched them come near and answered, "The word spread that the Apache are after you. You best get your gear and be gone from here."

Gabe looked at the man, "I thought this town was at peace with the Apache?"

"We are. That's why we want you gone. They're just as likely to come in here after you and forget all about that peace we have. So, all I can say is, *Vaya con Dios.*" He turned his back, stripped off his apron, lay it across the anvil, and walked away.

Gabe watched the man leave, went to the corner of the lean-to and grabbed the saddle and went to the corral for Ebony. Wolf had made himself at home with the horses, probably unseen by the smitty, and now stood to watch Gabe approach. Ezra was behind him and asked, "So, now what?"

"Well, we like travelin' at night, so, let's do it."

15 / BUTTE

The curtain of darkness hid the remaining light of dusk as Gabe and Ezra rode from the small village. The less than half moon did its best to light their way on the well-worn ancient trail. The tradesmen had made the wide trail to and from the village and the Pueblo of the Tewa people. The Tewa had been trading with others long before the Spaniards and others settled the village, which was the first appointed capital of the Spanish Territory, but now was a sleepy village with few businesses. The adobe walls and multi-level adobe pueblo stood like a shadowy beacon in the dim light, the flat-top structures, each with ladders leading to the upper levels, butt ends of roof timbers protruding above darkened doorways.

Nearby, a low burning cookfire cast shadows among the cottonwoods by the river and a figure walked from the shelter of the trees to confront the two riders. A familiar voice spoke, "Maiku," and Gabe recognized Slow Turtle. He stepped close, "I expected you to come. Once the people of the village knew you saw the Apache, they would want you gone."

"Surprised us, but we understand," replied Gabe. "Is your trade with the Tewa good?"

"Yes, but there will be more in the days to come. Some have to gather their goods," answered Turtle, then added, "Have you decided how you will go to Santa Fe?"

"Not particular. Just figgered we'd go south and follow the most used trail."

Turtle grinned, turned to face south, "Go downriver until you see a tall flat-top, black butte across the river, there is a good crossing with a gravel bar island. After you cross, follow the stream toward the rising sun until a smaller stream comes from the far side. There you will find the trail of the ancients. Follow that, probably beside a dry bed, all the way to Santa Fe."

"What about the Apache? We were told your Caputa Ute are friends with the *Olleros.*"

"Our leaders have talked about joining the Apache in the fight against the Comanche but our band has not joined them."

Gabe nodded, "Maybe we will see you in Santa Fe?"

"We will not be there for some time; my woman has friends here."

"Then we will go. Don't want those Apache catching up to us."

Slow Turtle lifted his head in a slow nod, stepped back and watched as Gabe and Ezra moved past. When Gabe looked back, Turtle lifted his hand in a wave and Gabe returned the gesture. The men rode side by side, the horses taking a brisk pace, hooves silent on the dusty trail. It was but a short while later when they spotted the large flat-top butte across the river and pushed their horses through the cottonwoods and willows to the riverbank. The muddy waters moved quietly, ripples rhythmically splashing against the bank and rocky gravel bar. Gabe stood in his stirrups looking across to the gravel bar island told of by Turtle and on to the sloping bank on the far side that told of the oft-used crossing. With a glance to Ezra, "Well, here goes!" and tossed the lead rope over the neck of the grey and nudged Ebony to the water. Wolf splashed in beside the stallion and started paddling against the strong current, angling toward the far shore. The current caught the big black and Gabe slipped from the saddle on the downstream side, keeping a grip on the tie-down straps beside the pommel and letting Ebony bob in the water, his feet often touching bottom, as he tread against the current, his nose stretched out before him.

The first channel was but fifty to sixty feet wide and Ebony soon had footing to climb the near bank of the gravel bar. Once on solid ground, the horse shook, looking like he wanted to roll but Gabe's taut hold on the rein kept him moving. The point of the gravel bar was a little wider than the first channel and Gabe stepped back into the saddle to nudge Ebony into the second, wider, but shallower channel. Once on the far bank, Gabe stepped down, slipped the Ferguson from the scabbard, checked the saddle pistols, and the Mongol bow in its oiled and tight case. All the weapons were dry but Gabe chose to reload the Ferguson and his belt pistol to ensure the powder was dry and the weapons dependable. Ezra did the same with his Lancaster and pistol and they were soon on the trail again.

Moving to the south toward the stream that merged with the Rio Bravo, they sided the stream until a major trail came from the north to cross the shallow creek just above the confluence of the two, then sided the wider almost dry creek bed, bound to the south. The terrain was low hills, sparsely covered with piñon, scrub oak, and lots of cacti. Cholla, prickly pear, yucca, and sage added variety to the bunch grass and buffalo grass that blanketed the flats. Gabe looked around, "Although it's pretty flat, at least we aren't as exposed as before. Those hills and buttes on either side and the few trees give some cover."

"Yeah. Makes a fella feel right safe, don't it?" answered Ezra, sarcastically. "Don't know which is more appealing, stand up and get shot, or dive behind some cactus and get poked! Course, we could always look for some rattlesnakes to play tag with!"

Gabe chuckled, "Well, aren't you a bundle of optimism!"

The trail bent to the south to cross the dry wash and they were surprised to see a trickle of water winding through the sandy bottom. Gabe reined up and stepped down, letting the horses have a drink of the murky water, then went to one knee to scoop up a handful for himself. Ezra was belly down, face in the water, just upstream of the bay and the mule who were nose deep. Ezra stood, wiped off his face and looked around, glanced at Gabe, and asked, "How far to Santa Fe, ya reckon?"

Gabe detected more to the question than was asked, "Dunno, why?"

Ezra put his hand to the back of his neck, moving his head around as he rubbed it, then looked at his friend. "Don't like it."

Gabe knew the premonitions of his friend were as dependable as the sun rising and when the Black Irish and Celtic Druid genes spoke, both knew to listen. Gabe casually stepped beside Ebony, and with his usual fluid movement, swung aboard the big black. He reached over for the lead rope on the grey and with a glance at Ezra, now aboard his bay, nodded and started across the sandy-bottomed creek bed. Moonlight bounced off the water and gave dim illumination to the dark shadows of the trees. The rolling hills were sparsely covered with the piñon and gnarly cedar giving ample space between the low-growing trees. The hooves whispered in the sand, Gabe holding a taut rein but feeling Ebony's tense muscles beneath him. Wolf was skittish, often looking over his shoulder. Within a few strides, they stepped onto the far bank, pushed into the scrub oak, and with a glance to Ezra, both men slapped legs to the horses and the animals hunched their backs as they dug hooves into the loose soil and lunged forward.

They lay low on the necks of the horses, manes whipping their faces, as Ebony followed the black shadow of Wolf twisting through the piñon and cedar. Hooves pounded the dirt and rocks, saddles creaked, and Gabe and Ezra spoke to their horses, giving them their head to find their own footing and path through the scattered trees. Before them, a slight hill rose in the dim moonlight but Wolf had kept to a trail that bent around the butte. As they rounded the shoulder of the hill, Gabe saw a thick cluster of trees sided by a rocky mound with scraggly cedar and quickly reined up, giving a whistle to call Wolf back, and slid the Ferguson from the scabbard as he swung down.

Behind them, the thunder of hooves and the screaming war cries of Apache warriors pierced the quiet of the night, screams that were intended to dispel the demons of darkness and drive fear into the hearts of their prey but only announced their nearness. Gabe motioned Wolf to stay with the horses, guarding them from the would-be horse thieves. Ezra slid the bay to a stop, his own feet hitting the ground before the animal finished his slide. Gabe had dropped behind a sizable boulder, lifted the Ferguson, and eared back the hammer to set the triggers. He took a breath, let it slowly escape as he centered the front blade on the dull white breastplate of the first warrior. He squeezed the trigger as the blade sight followed the target. The rifle roared and bucked, fire stabbed into the darkness, the big weapon spitting smoke and lead, and the warrior bent forward but slid backward off the rump of his running horse. Other warriors reined their mounts to the side as Ezra's Lancaster flared its own lance of flame and blasted to unseat another warrior.

Gabe lifted the Bailes over/under pistol, cocking the hammer as he brought the sight to bear and fired. The lance of fire filled Gabe with the sense of power as if bearing the shaft of lightning and another warrior blossomed red but grabbed a handful of mane and lay on his mount's neck as he turned into the trees. As Gabe rotated the barrels for another shot, he heard Ezra's pistol bark and he searched for another target. The small band of warriors had passed the promontory of Gabe and

Ezra but the handful that remained turned their horses and charged back toward the two men.

Gabe's pistol roared, the flame showing his position, prompting Gabe to duck behind the boulder just as arrows clattered among the rocks behind him. Yet from his sheltered position, he heard the first warrior scream when the big lead ball plowed a furrow down his back. The man had lain low on the neck of his horse but the bullet found its mark and the warrior, whose spine had been shattered, slid to the ground and tumbled end over end to land on his face, unmoving. Ezra's second barrel also barked and found its mark, driving the round ball through the neck of another man, unseating him, and painting the dry soil with his blood that showed black in the dim moonlight.

The thunder of hooves lessened and the trees were stilled with a blanket of silence. But the bitter smell of burnt powder filled the quiet air and the stench of blood and death followed. The two friends could hear the other breathe and they looked at one another as Gabe whispered, "You all right?"

"Yeah, you?" answered Ezra as he started reloading his weapons.

Gabe was busy with his Ferguson, quickly finished and reloaded both barrels of the Bailes pistol, jammed it into his belt and said, "Let's move!" He deftly and quietly moved to Ebony, who stood silently beside the grey, Wolf had come to his feet, looking at his returning friends and stepped forward for the reassurance of Gabe's hand on his scruff. With a quick stroke of Wolf's fur, Gabe stepped aboard Ebony and with a glance to Ezra, the men moved into the trees, pointing south with the north star at their back, looking for the easy-going trail they left behind.

Wolf walked beside Ebony while Ezra and his bay were on the other side. They had easily found the trail and were bound for Santa Fe yet watching their back trail as often as they looked to the south in hopes of seeing some sign of Santa Fe. With no other encounters with the Apache, they soon sighted the rising hills that seemed to crowd the trail, but within a few miles, they crested the timbered hills and looked down on the dark buildings of the settlement. Ezra said, "You don't think they'd try anything this close to town, do ya?"

Gabe reined up, leaned on the pommel, and turned to look at Ezra, "What makes you think I know any more about the Apache than you do?" A glimmer of light to his left brought his attention to the silhouetted mountains that lifted their jagged dark peaks to frame the coming morning's light. The sky showed a hint of gold as a promise of a new day. Gabe looked at Ezra for his answer.

With a chuckle and a grin, as much of relief as they looked at the village below and no one behind them, he muttered, "I dunno. You always act like you know everything, I just figgered . . ."

Gabe shook his head and gigged Ebony on, glanced to his left and saw the first colors glowing brighter with the coming of morning and smiled, "I'm thinkin' I'd like to find a fine cantina and have some breakfast, what say you?"

"Now you're speakin' my language!" declared Ezra, laughing with his friend.

16 / SANTA FE

The trail came from the northeast as it dropped into the valley from the rolling hills. When the hills pushed back, Gabe and Ezra found themselves facing farm fields, many with corn high as Wolf's belly, others showing a variety of crops, some with a different plant in every row. The farmer's cottages varied only by size, each one a flat-top adobe hut or home. Most had small barns or a lean-to for the animals, corrals holding oxen, burros, or mules. The trail was now a well-used roadway, carts and wagons cutting ruts and broadening the way. The sun was beginning to show its face above the eastern mountains, bending its lances of light across the valley and the village. They passed a peasant farmer leading a burro pulling a two-wheel cart loaded with tall clay containers that sloshed fresh milk about. As they passed, Gabe asked, "Estable?"

"Si, si! *Debajo de la plaza,*" he answered, waving his arm to the south toward the river.

"Gracias," answered Gabe, giving a slight wave to the wrinkled old farmer. He turned to Ezra, "That's easy enough. Just below the plaza, toward the river, we'll find the stable."

"I'd rather find a cantina!" mumbled Ezra.

Gabe chuckled and nudged Ebony to a trot. As they neared the settlement, Gabe reined back to a walk. They passed a two-story structure with a cross atop and a sign near the door that identified the building as a Convent of Saint Francisco. The road divided and Gabe chose the branch that pointed to the river hoping to find the stable. There were more cornfields behind the buildings and beside the roadway but Gabe saw a sizable building at the corner of a field near the river. As they came near, they saw a man opening double doors that revealed the interior of a stable and blacksmith shop. The man was more of a big boy, barefoot, linen trousers that were above his ankles and held at his waist with a rope, a linen vest that hung open, but his shoulders and upper arms showed developing muscles. The young man turned at the sound of horses, smiled and said, "Bienvenidos hombres!"

Gabe grinned and answered in Spanish, "Morning. We need a place for our horses and maybe a place to sleep for ourselves."

"Si, si. The horses can be in the corral or in a stall inside if you wish. You can take a stall or sleep in the loft." He looked from the men to the horses, "And your saddles and gear will be safe with us, also." He paused, looked at Gabe and Ezra, "Stalls for the horses, two pesos, for you, two pesos, if you sleep in the same stall." He frowned when he saw Wolf come from between the horses, "He sleep with you?"

Gabe grinned, looked at Ezra, "You gonna snore?"

"Of course. That's how you know I'm sleeping."

Gabe looked back at the young man, nodding, "Yes, he," pointing to Wolf, "will sleep with us and we'll want to be near the horses and our gear." Gabe flipped the young man a coin, "We'll leave the packhorses now but we'll go into town to eat. A good cantina?" he asked.

The young man caught the coin, looked at it and smiled, looked back at Gabe, "Si. The Cantina Santa Fe in the plaza. *Muy buena*!" he declared.

They stripped the gear from all the horses, rubbed them down with a brush provided by the stable boy, and decided to walk back to the plaza for their breakfast. They stashed their weapons under some loose hay beneath the stack of gear and saddles and, with only the Bailes over/under pistols in their belts, they started to the plaza, thinking only of a good meal at the cantina.

The first street that led to the plaza was at the fork

beside the convent. They stepped onto a covered boardwalk that fronted a long low adobe building with several different merchants or businesses, many busy at sweeping the walkway or opening for the day. Several greeted Gabe and Ezra as they passed, all staring curiously at the newcomers that were not Spanish or Indian. At the end of the first long building, the plaza opened up and Gabe and Ezra stopped to take in the unusual sight. It was the first town or business place Ezra had seen since they left Philadelphia and for Gabe since he left St. Louis. The plaza was a square park-like setting separated by a narrow roadway from the surrounding adobe buildings. To their left was a church building, business on either side, directly before them and lining the entire west side was another long building with a covered walkway that showed signs of several merchants. On the north edge, rose an impressive building that they would discover was the home of the governor. The east side showed several individual structures adjoined and sharing a common, covered walkway. "Didn't that boy say the cantina was over here," suggested Ezra, nodding to the east side of the plaza.

"I believe so," answered Gabe, stepping off the walkway and crossing the narrow street. Two doors from the corner they spotted the swinging sign, *Cantina Santa Fe,* and with a grin, Ezra led the way into the delightful smelling business. They stopped just inside the door, letting their eyes become accustomed to the lesser light, and noticed several tables already held hungry customers. An attractive and aproned woman waved them to a table beside a window and in the corner. She smiled as she greeted them, looked at Ezra with a critical eye and an upraised eyebrow, then back to Gabe as they were seated. She spoke in Spanish as she explained, "We have huevos rancheros or anything else you would like."

Ezra spoke up, "Just bring us a big plate full of your best, whatever it may be, and coffee if you have it." He smiled as he patted his belly, "I'm so hungry my belly's pinching my backbone!" He shook his head as he laughed but sobered quickly as he saw his words did not please the woman.

"I apologize for my friend. He just likes to eat and it's been a while since we've had a good meal. So, whatever you have, just bring plenty of it and he'll be happy."

After the woman left, Gabe frowned at Ezra, "I'm not sure it was your words or her understanding that was the problem."

Before Ezra could respond, the woman returned with big mugs of steaming coffee and set one before each of the men. As she glanced at Ezra, he said, "I apologize ma'am. I meant no offense. Please forgive my rudeness."

She let a slow smile cross her face as she looked

from Ezra to Gabe and explained, "It was not your words, señor. I have never seen a man like you before and I was, well, surprised."

"I understand. Forgive me."

"Si, señor," she replied and turned away to fetch their order.

When she returned, she had two large platters of food and a smaller basket with hot tortillas. Both men smiled and after a quick word of thanks to the Lord, they began work on the feast of eggs, strips of steak, vegetables, rice, beans, and more. By the time the plates were empty and they finished the coffee, both were well satisfied, and sat back to relax. They were enjoying a fresh cup of coffee when a man approached them who appeared to be Spanish but was attired in buckskins similar to Gabe and Ezra. "Pardon me, señors, but I could not help but notice you are visitors to our town. Allow me to introduce myself, I am known as Pedro Vial although my name is Pierre Vial. And let me bid you welcome. Will you be with us long?"

Gabe motioned for him to join them and answered, "I am Gabe and this is Ezra," nodding to Ezra, "and no, we will not be here long. Just a day or so to get re-supplied and we'll leave."

"Oh, I'm sorry señor, I did not mean to be intrusive. I just noticed you are in buckskins like me and I thought we might have similar interests. Are you trappers?"

"No, not trappers. But we have been doin' a bit of travelin' around, meetin' folks, here and there. Some friendly, some not so."

"I've just returned recently from some traveling myself. Spent a couple years in St. Louis but the west is better." He nodded to the woman as she placed a cup of coffee before him and he looked at Gabe, "You?"

"Just runnin' from some Apache north of here a ways."

Vial frowned, "That's odd. The Jicarilla Apache have been at peace for some time. Perhaps they were some renegades."

"They weren't too peaceful with the Escalante Hacienda. After we found them slaughtered, we tried to convince the Apache to leave us alone but they took a little convincing. Not real sure they've learned yet."

"For quite some time, it was the Comanche that were the problem but we've made peace with them. It is troublesome, what you say."

"You've been with the Comanche?" asked Gabe.

"Yes, I have lived with them and brokered the peace with them."

"Which Comanche?"

Vial cocked his head to the side as he looked at Gabe, "You know the Comanche?'

"Some."

"Several bands of the Kotsoteka Comanche, the eastern Comanche."

"I spent some time with the Yaparuhka Comanche recently. Old Owl is their chief."

The men paused in their conversation, considering one another, and enjoying their coffee until Gabe asked, "So, catch us up on the happenings of the country. Who's president of the states now?"

Vial smiled, "Jefferson. And when did you last 'catch up' on the happenings?"

"Oh, let me see," he glanced at Ezra, frowning, "maybe three, four years now."

Vial frowned, "You have been in the mountains that long?"

"No, longer. Spent time with several different tribes, from the Osage to the Gros Ventre, Crow, Arapaho, Shoshone, Kutenai, and others. But tell us about things," urged Gabe.

Vial lifted his eyebrows as he thought, "You know the Spanish Louisiana?"

"Yes, seen most of it."

"The most recent is that the Spanish have traded it to the French and the French just sold it to the States."

Gabe frowned, "All that?"

Vial nodded, grinning, leaned forward and lowered his voice, "But the Spanish here do not want to recognize that the territory is not theirs, so be careful what you say." He sat back, grinning, "And there has been talk that Jefferson will sent an exploratory group to map the territory."

Gabe shook his head, glancing from Ezra to Vial, "That's all we need is a bunch of settlers and such coming out from the east and thinking they can put farms and towns ever which where!"

Gabe looked at Vial, "So, when you came back from St. Louis, overland or . . .?

Vial answered, "Missouri River to Westport, west across country to Arkansas River, southwest to Santa Fe," he stated, smiling as he sat back. "The Pawnee were the most difficult but the Kansa or Kaw were friendly."

Gabe looked at Ezra, grinning, "Pawnee, difficult. Ummhmm."

The men looked at one another understanding as only those that had been through that country and met those people could understand. Gabe said, "So, tell us about the Apache. They have been anything but friendly."

Vial said, "They are a unique people. They can be friendly, good traders, great horsemen, valiant fighters. But they can also be cruel and vicious. I have seen them skin a captive alive, cutting thin strips of skin off the chest and arms as their captive screamed. They will be friends with one village and not with another. Raid their enemies, steal their women and children, and sell them to the friendly village. But if there is a band of renegades or not, if they consider you their enemy, they will never let up until they have their vengeance or more." He paused, looked from Gabe to Ezra, "What put them onto you?"

Gabe sipped his coffee, set it down, and explained, "We came on the Escalante hacienda, saw the mutilated bodies, but also saw them watching us from the hillside. We hightailed it, saw 'em across the river and tried to warn them off. Wounded one, maybe killed another. They followed us, hit us 'bout five, six miles north of here last night. We killed another five or six before we took off again, they didn't follow."

Vial nodded, looking from Gabe to Ezra, "They probably have someone in the hills watching for you even now. Do you know how big the party was that raided the hacienda?"

"Maybe twenty or so," answered Ezra.

"The Apache are not foolish. When the cost is too great, they will not readily lose more. But they are also a vengeful people. They have marked you as enemies and if they believe they can take you or destroy you without great loss, they will do so. It will give great honor to whoever can bring that vengeance for the people. If they are not a band of renegades and are part of a bigger village, it could be even worse for you."

"That doesn't sound very good. We've got families to go home to and we can't get there without going through their country," surmised Gabe, finishing his coffee. "But for now, we need to get some rest 'fore we return for our supplies. It has been good visiting with you Señor Vial. Perhaps we will visit again before we leave."

The men stood, shook hands and Vial watched as Gabe and Ezra left the cantina. Gabe glanced over his shoulder as he walked through the doorway and stopped on the covered walkway. "What say we walk around the plaza and locate a trading post or mercantile store for our supplies?"

"Sounds reasonable," drawled Ezra. Both men were thinking about their return through Apache territory and whispered prayers as they walked.

17 / TRADER

"That's why the people of Santa Fe believe themselves safe from an Indian attack!" declared Gabe, nodding to the fortified walls behind the governor's palace.

"What you reckon they have, a couple hundred soldiers there?" asked Ezra. The men had chosen to make a circuitous ride about the village before going to the traders for supplies.

"Prob'ly. If those walls hold barracks, I'd say at least that many." He glanced to the embrasured towers situated at the corners of the square pueblo-looking structure. "Looks to be about a hundred-foot square, prob'ly has a central compound and offices for the commander and such. So, yeah, I'd say at least a couple hundred."

"We didn't see any of 'em in the plaza yesterday. You think they ever let 'em out?" asked Ezra as they took the narrow roadway that pointed to the plaza.

"Oh, I'm sure they get out ever now and then. Mighta just been busy. We'll prob'ly see some today," answered Gabe, turning Ebony into the plaza and taking the roadway between the plaza and the businesses on the east side. He nodded toward the open doorway beneath the swinging sign, *Comerciante,* with smaller letters beneath, *Suministros y Bienes.* Ezra looked at the sign, back at Gabe, "What's that say?"

Gabe chuckled, "Trader, Supplies and Goods."

Ezra laughed, "Guess that's what we want."

They stopped, stepped down and flipped the reins over the hitch rail, secured the lead ropes of the packhorse and mule beside the horses, and with a wave of his hand, Gabe motioned Wolf to stay with the horses. The men stepped through the doorway, stopped to let their eyes become accustomed to the light and were assaulted by the many aromas of the trading post. The post also served as an inn of sorts, three tables were arrayed near the single fly specked window, only one had men, all three in the uniform of the Mexican garrison. Leather, oils, sweat, hides all added to the smell and when Gabe stepped to the counter, the man behind the planks was the most aromatic of all.

"Ah, señors! What do you need?" he asked, grinning and showing both of his brown teeth. His whiskered face was pock marked, his eyes bloodshot, and his single eyebrow almost covered his eyes. A few random black hairs valiantly tried to cover his dome but to no avail. His grimy shirt hung open to expose more hair on his chest, matted with the droppings of his previous meals, and his ham hock hands rested on the counter. Gabe turned his head slightly to try to avoid the stench but was unsuccessful. He said, "We need some supplies."

"Si, si. I can help you with that. Do you have a list?"

Gabe looked up at the man, "Write it down as I say it, and we'll wait."

"Si, si. But I do not have to write it down, just tell me."

"Twenty pounds of sugar, twenty pounds of coffee, twenty pounds of cornmeal . . ." he began and watched as the man hurriedly began stacking bags on the counter. He continued with the rest of his list, watching, and waiting. Ezra asked, "Shall I start loadin'?"

The clerk quickly answered, "No, no. Wait until I can make the tally," and continued gathering goods. Ezra nodded, stepped away from the counter and went to a table to wait. A shadow darkened the doorway and Ezra looked up to see two men, both uniformed step into the room, pause and look around at everyone. One of the two, with an insignia and several red hash marks on the sleeve of his blue uniform jacket, nodded to the other whose uniform suggested he was an officer with epaulets on his shoulders, braided trim on the bill of his cap, some medals on his chest and with his red britches tucked into high topped shiny leather boots. The officer stood stiffly erect, raised one eyebrow as he sneered at Ezra then stepped toward him.

"You! Why are you here?" barked the officer, stepping near the table.

His stern remark caught Gabe's attention, who turned to look at the man. The officer snarled again, "Answer me!" as he touched the hilt of his scabbarded saber.

Ezra looked up at the man, glanced at Gabe, and answered, "We're gettin' supplies."

"Stand when you address your superiors!" demanded the officer, glaring at the seated Ezra.

Ezra frowned, looked around the room, glanced at Gabe with a touch of a grin, then back to the officer. "I don't see any superiors!" growled Ezra, his eyes narrowing and the muscles in his cheeks and neck flexing as he glared at the man.

The officer's eyes widened, his nostrils flared, and he glanced to the man that came in with him, nodded for him to come to the table. He growled at the sergeant, motioning toward Ezra, "Put this man in irons!" The sergeant looked from the officer to Ezra, started to move toward him but was stopped by a voice from behind him.

"I wouldn't do that!" declared Gabe, intentionally keeping his voice level as he faced the two soldiers.

"This is none of your affair!" shouted the officer and nodded to the sergeant again.

The man stepped closer to Ezra but Ezra stood and with his hand on the butt of his pistol, he growled at the sergeant, "Don't even think about it!" The sergeant stopped, looking at the determined stare of Ezra and looked back at the officer.

Before the officer could say anything, Gabe stepped closer, "Just what do you think you are doing?" he asked.

The officer noticed Gabe's hand on his pistol, glanced back at Ezra, and returned his snarl towards Gabe, "Is this *negro* your slave?"

"This *man* is a free man and my brother!"

"You have no right to interfere in the business of the *Alcalde*!"

"You and your *Alcalde* have no business with us! Now, since we are not a part of your garrison, nor a part of this," he looked around, nodding with his head, "settlement. We'll get our supplies and will leave your business to you and your soldier boys!" Gabe had slowly stepped between the officer and Ezra as he spoke and now stood with his face inches away from the officer's. He knew he had backed the man up in front of his men and he would be forced to either eat crow or try to assume more authority. Gabe waited, watching the fury grow in the man's eyes, as he looked from side to side.

He stepped away from Gabe and looked at Ezra, "How can you be free? Did you exercise *coartación*?"

Gabe stepped closer again and answered, "No, he did not have to exercise the right of self-purchase. He was free born! He is not now a slave, nor has he ever been a slave!"

Ezra stepped around the table, coming to Gabe's side, and looked at his friend and nodded. Then looked at the officer, "There are many men of my color that are in this country and are free. Your soldier outfit has complete garrisons of men of color and yet you question my being free. Why?"

The officer stuttered as he backed up, looked at the three soldiers who had been watching the happenings, and ordered the sergeant, "Get those men back to the garrison! Now!"

The sergeant turned, motioned to the men, "You heard the lieutenant! Move!" The men scrambled to their feet and crowded one another as they pushed through the door, followed closely by the sergeant. When they cleared the doorway, another man stepped into the room, glanced at the officer and Gabe and Ezra. He spoke up, "Ah, Lieutenant, I see you have met my friends, the adventurers from the north, Gabe and Ezra."

Gabe grinned as he recognized Pedro Vial, "Pedro! Good to see you again. We were just having a friendly chat with the officer here," nodding to the soldier. He glanced from Vial to the Lieutenant, saw the recognition and immediate servient response of the man, then looked back at a grinning Vial.

The lieutenant turned back to face Gabe and Ezra, touched the brim of his cap with a stiff salute, bent slightly at the waist, and turned on his heels and followed his men. Vial stepped close and spoke in low tones, "That man has been rumored to be dealing in captives and slaves. Watch your back." He touched Gabe on his shoulder and walked from the room.

Gabe looked at Ezra, who was leaning on the table, fuming, and shaking his head. Gabe slapped his hand on Ezra's back, "Let's get our stuff and make tracks!"

"It is good that you leave quickly, *señors*. The lieutenant is not a man to back down and to be seen by his men as if he did, is not good. He is not a good man to cross," stated the clerk, hurriedly gathering the rest of their supplies. The counter was stacked high with bags and goods, as well as a stack beside the counter. He began fidgeting with a tattered piece of paper and a piece of charcoal as he tallied their goods.

When Ezra asked if he could start loading, the clerk nodded, continuing with his calculating. When he finished, he looked up and sheepishly said, "Sixteen pesos?"

Gabe grinned, fumbled in his pockets and withdrew two gold coins, one slightly smaller, but both had a Liberty cap figure on one side and a small eagle on the other. He put them on the counter, "That one," pointing at the larger coin, "is ten dollars and the other is five dollars. That's fifteen dollars which is about the same, maybe a little more than your pesos." He looked up at the clerk who was smiling and nodding.

"Si, si, *señor,* but I said *sixteen* pesos."

Gabe nodded, reached back into his pocket and brought out a silver dollar, which was bigger and heavier than the gold coins, placed it on the counter and looked at the man. "Sixteen."

The clerk smiled broadly and quickly gathered the coins and stuffed them into his pocket. He looked at Gabe, "Let me help you with your things, you must leave!" He reached for the lead ingots and started to the door. Within a short while, the packs were secured and Gabe and Ezra swung aboard and started from the plaza.

"With the garrison thataway," stated Gabe, nodding toward the governor's palace, "how 'bout we go thataway?" nodding toward the southeast corner where they first entered the plaza the day before. He did not wait for an answer but turned Ebony toward the narrow roadway and, within moments, they were moving between the many cornfields and aiming for the rolling hills north of Santa Fe.

18 / AMBUSH

"So, are we getting out of the fryin' pan and into the fire?" asked Ezra as they neared the edge of the cornfield.

Gabe turned to look at his friend, frowning, "You thinkin' 'bout what Pedro Vial said?"

"Yeah, but also rememberin' what he said about the Apache. For all we know, they're watching right now!" he looked around to emphasize his concern. Ezra shrugged, rolling his shoulders and scanned behind them, "And I'm gettin' that feelin'. . ." With a quick glance to Gabe, Ezra slapped legs to the big bay just as arrows whispered between them. He hunkered down in the saddle as the bay lunged forward, took a dally of the lead of the mule around the saddle horn and felt the line grow taut across his thigh, but slackened quickly as the mule matched the bay stride for stride.

Gabe, Ebony, and the grey were beside Ezra as the horses dug deep and stretched out. The sun was lowering in the west and dusk would soon lower its curtain but the remaining light was enough as Wolf led the way, twisting through the sparse junipers and piñons. The men lay low on the horses' necks, legs clinging tightly as the animals made their way over the rolling terrain. At the bottom of a wide gulley, Wolf jogged to the side and ran, keeping to the sandy bottom. The horses' hooves that had clattered over the rocks and gravely hillsides now whispered in the loose sand, the only sounds the creak of saddle leather and the grunting of the horses. Dull thuds marked each step and it became obvious the horses were working harder to make way in the deep sand.

Gabe frowned, knowing something was different, and slowly lifted his head, turning and looking behind them. The war cries had diminished and no other sound of pursuit came. He pulled Ebony back to an easy canter, then to a walk. Ezra slowed his bay and sat erect, also twisting around, searching behind and beside them. They were in a shallow gulley but they could see over the banks and there was no sign of the Apache. They were at least ten miles from Santa Fe and the trees were giving way to sage and cacti. Ezra was almost afraid to ask, thinking that to suggest what he hoped would take away the possibility. But he spoke just loud enough for Gabe to hear,

"You think we lost 'em?"

"Dunno. Sounds like it, but . . ."

"Yeah, can't trust 'em," added Ezra, finishing Gabe's thought.

"Let's keep goin' a spell, then we'll stop and check with the scope."

Wolf stood watching the others, waiting for them to come, and sat down to wait. As his friends neared, he glanced from them to the mouth of the ravine, back at Gabe as if to ask, "Which way," and continued his loping trot to the open end of the gulley. He stopped and waited for them to come near, knowing the habit of Gabe to find a high point and climb atop for a look-see, and he was right. The men reined up beside a pair of juniper at the base of a long sloping hog-back ridge and Gabe stepped down. With his rifle in one hand and the cased scope hanging from his shoulder, he motioned to Wolf to lead the way. Ezra sat down near the juniper, leaned back against the slope, and pushed his hat over his eyes as he stretched out.

The animals stood side by side, Ebony was ground tied and the grey, usually on free rein, stood beside the black, lead line thrown over his neck. The bay stood on the far side of Ezra, the mule behind him, his lead line still tethered to the saddle horn on the bay's saddle. The animals' sides were heaving and they shifted their weight from leg to leg. Nostrils flared as they breathed deep, ears twitched as their sweat moistened manes and sides absorbed the cooler air of the soon coming evening.

As Ezra lay, stretching out his legs, thinking of the cantina back in Santa Fe, his thoughts wandered to the conversation they had with Pedro Vial. He remembered the man describing the Apache, "These Apache are different from any other natives I've known. The Osage, Kaw, Pawnee, and Comanche are all wily warriors but the Apache are the greatest fighters I've known." He paused, squirmed in his seat as he thought about them, "They can be a few feet in front of you, the only thing around some scrub sage or cactus, and you can't see him. They can be in the open desert and you would swear there wasn't a living thing out there and, before you know it, dozens of 'em will come up outta the sand and come charging at you. They can move without so much as a whisper of the wind. And they're smart! They won't keep coming if they're takin' losses. They value their own more than an enemy and will do everything to keep from losing even a single warrior. And if you get in a tangle with 'em, don't turn your back or quit until he's dead, because he will keep coming and coming. There is no quit in 'em!"

The thoughts of Vial made Ezra catch his breath at a whisper of movement. He was certain it was just the horses but he reached for his hat and began to sit up and was clubbed to the side of the head. Darkness blanketed him and he felt he was falling, his arms flailing to the sides but feeling nothing, excruciating pain beating at his head as his face hit the sand, and he fought for air, but dust filled his nostrils and sand covered his lips, and his consciousness failed him.

Gabe and Wolf angled up the side of the slope, found a cut in the rimrock and struggled to the crest of the ridge. The sun had dropped below the western mountains and he knew he would be difficult to spot in the fading light but he bellied down and crawled to the edge of the rimrock, Wolf at his side. He stretched out the scope, looking around as he began to adjust it, then with it at his eye, he scanned their backtrail. He slowly worked his scan back up the gulley, searching the banks and flats beside it, carefully examining every cluster of trees, every jumble of rocks, any and every place that could hide a band of Apache. He was bringing the scan closer, looking to either side of the gulley when Wolf growled and came to his feet. He was looking almost directly below them when Gabe saw movement.

War cries and screams suddenly filled the air as horses and riders came from behind the scattered trees and gullies, every dip in the terrain seemed to sprout Apaches. Gabe rose to one knee, lifting his rifle to his shoulder, looking for a target. But before he could center on a single warrior, the dust rose from below and the entire band was on the run away from the ridge. And he saw what he feared, Ezra's bay and the mule and across the saddle of the bay was a body in buckskins and Gabe knew it was his friend. The last of the warriors were fighting with the grey packhorse but it reared up and jerked the lead line from the man's hand, almost unseating him. The others were shouting and gesturing toward the retreating band and they left the grey and took to the trail after the others.

Gabe frowned and searched the trees for his black, but the dust was thick, the light dim and the scattered juniper and gullies obscured his view. He ran to the cut in the rimrock, followed Wolf as he slid down the narrow opening on his rump, then came to his feet and bounded down the steep slope. Within moments, he was at the spot where they stopped, saw Ezra's floppy felt hat and went to pick it up. Blood showed on the brim but he saw none on the ground. *That's good, he wasn't bleeding too bad. And they wouldn't take a dead man.* The thought that Ezra was now a captive of the Apache and wounded, kindled the rage in Gabe's gut. He looked at the tracks where Ebony had stood, saw them cut around the tree and showed he left in a hurry. Gabe scanned the area, wondering if any of the warriors were left behind for him. He bent beside Wolf, whispered, "Apache, look for 'em!" and motioned by moving his arm in a circle around the area. Wolf trotted off, head below his shoulders and moving side to side. Gabe stood and climbed the edge of the gulley, moving in the same direction as the tracks of his black.

He had brought the Ferguson to full cock when he was atop the ridge but lowered the hammer as he slid down the slope. Now he eared back the hammer, watching and listening. The whisper of a branch of sage on buckskin, a sound most would not hear or recognize, brought Gabe around and he fired the big Ferguson from the hip at the startled warrior. The man had his war club raised and was about to lunge at Gabe but the .62 caliber lead ball that took him in his belly stopped him. The man crumpled like a thrown-away rag doll as the big ball exited his back, taking a sizable portion of his backbone with it. Gabe grabbed at his pistol as another warrior came at him, his lance held high, but Gabe leaped to the side, cocking the Bailes pistol as he did and let the ball loose. The pistol roared and billowed smoke. The warrior came through the smoke like a ship through the fog, his high masted lance wavering above. But the ball had torn away the man's jaw and burrowed into his skull. His momentum had carried him a few steps but now he fell on his face, the lance impaling itself in a cluster of prickly pear cactus.

Gabe had fallen on his shoulder and he quickly squirmed around and came to his feet, rotating the barrels on the pistol as he did. He brought the hammer to full cock, glanced at the second pan and frizzen to be certain it was closed and ready, then searched the dim light for any other movement. Wolf trotted from behind a cluster of juniper, acting as if nothing had happened and even appearing to smile. Gabe shook his head as he started to speak to the wolf but movement behind him revealed the big black stallion striding toward him, head high, keeping the trailing reins from under foot.

Gabe chuckled, bent down and stroked Wolf's head and scruff, "Good boy! Good boy!"

He stepped to Ebony, lifted the reins, and ran his fingers over Ebony's face and neck, talking to his friend, thankful for the animal being a one-man horse. He remembered his Pa saying, "Even I can't get near that beast! He is more of a one-man horse than any I've ever seen!" Gabe remembered other times when would-be horse thieves had made a try at the black, only to be bitten, kicked, run over, or trampled. The only ones that had ridden the black besides himself were the times he had doubled up with his sons and once with Cougar Woman.

He checked his weapons, the two saddle pistols still rested in the holsters beside the pommel, the cased Mongol bow was under the left stirrup fender, the quiver of arrows hung at the far side behind the cantle, and his bedroll was still intact. He reloaded the Ferguson and the Bailes over/under pistol, slipped the rifle in the scabbard and stuffed the pistol in his belt and swung aboard. He grabbed at his pistol when he heard something coming from the draw but the familiar head of the grey bobbed as he climbed from the ravine and came to stand beside the black, his packs intact. Gabe leaned over to touch the grey on his face and rub behind his ears, then reached down and patted the black's neck, motioned to Wolf, "We've got it to do boys, so let's go."

19 / CHASE

With but a nod, Gabe sent Wolf on the trail after the fleeing Apache. From what he had seen and the number of tracks, he guessed there were about a dozen, maybe fifteen, in the bunch. With a glance off his left shoulder, he saw the fading glow of the sun and dusk had exhausted its supply of light. The heavenly bodies were lighting their lanterns and, to his right, he saw the rocking cradle of the sliver of moon. His eyes were adjusting to the darkness. He knew the horses were tired and would need to be spared as much as possible but he feared for the safety of Ezra. He frowned as he thought of the actions of the Apache to take Ezra as a captive, especially after the previous fights when they had killed many of the raiders. Usually, most natives would seek retribution or vengeance against an enemy warrior that would include considerable torture. He shook his head as he thought that might be their purpose, a torturous death. But he also knew most natives respected a strong enemy and admired their fighting ability but that did not mean mercy. *We've got to find him soon,* whispered Gabe, if only to reassure himself.

The monotonous terrain was littered with sparse juniper, piñon, cedar, mesquite, and cacti galore. With innumerable ridges, ravines, gullies, dry washes, rolling hills, he could not understand the route taken by the Apache. The only consistency to their travel was a basic bent to the north. Where Ezra was taken, the raiders crossed a small creek and had stopped at a bosque just below the ridge, watered their horses and drank deeply themselves. The tracks of horses and knee prints of men told the story and Gabe had done the same. But that had been more than an hour past and the dusty hills and trail had robbed both man and horse of moisture. Wolf led them down a dry wash amidst several flat-top ridges that brought them into a wider arroyo with greenery. Hoping for a clear water stream, Ebony picked up the pace and followed Wolf into the willows and cottonwoods but the stream bed held but a trickle of water.

Gabe stepped down and worked quickly moving away rocks and stacking them together to make a pool for the water to gather. He stepped back and watched the trickle fill the declivity, and let the horses take their drink. As they lifted their heads and looked for grass, Gabe dropped the reins and let Ebony move to the grassy bank with the grey close behind.

Gabe lifted his arms high, bent backwards to stretch his back, and looked around for any sign of their prey. As he waited for the water to pool and clear, he walked upstream several yards and found the crossing made by the Apache. It appeared they made no effort to water their animals nor themselves but crossed without stopping. *Well, that tells me one of two things. Either they're gettin' close to their camp, or a better source of water. The Apache might be able to go great distances without water, but horses have to drink.*

He walked back to the horses, went to a knee beside the now cleared water and scooped several handfuls to quench his thirst. He went to Ebony, shook his water bag to ensure it was full, and swung aboard. With a wave to Wolf, they were again on the trail. But a short distance from the crossing, Wolf stopped, looking toward the retreating sign, but turning to look across the flats to a low rolling ridge. As Gabe came near, he stepped down to examine the tracks in the dim light, searching for what had prompted Wolf to stop and as Wolf moved away from the trail, Gabe noted the tracks of two horses that split from the others, one going to the right, the other opposite. Gabe slowly stood, wary and casually looking around, listening, but the only sound was the cry of a distant coyote and the anxious movement of the horses. He looked at Ebony whose neck was craned to the side, head lifted, and ears pricked as he looked into the darkness, but the Grey had turned the other way, his stance much the same and seemed to be looking toward a slight draw.

Gabe stepped beside Ebony, casually slipping one of the saddle pistols from its holster and attempted to muffle the sound of cocking the hammers as he held it close to his belly and coughed as he eared back both hammers. Wolf had disappeared into a small cluster of juniper that sat beside a stack of rocks and cactus. Gabe drew a slow breath, his back to Ebony, and searched the shadowy trees and sage for any movement. He heard the sound of a bowstring sliding from the fingers of a warrior, the string drawing taut and emitting a slight twang followed by the whisper of an arrow. Gabe instantly dropped to one knee, the arrow impaling itself in the thick leather of the saddle seat just above his head. He quickly moved away from Ebony, afraid another arrow might strike the horse, and stepped beside the pile of rocks, leaning behind the largest for cover. Another arrow whispered past, followed by the screaming charge of a warrior, war club uplifted in one hand, a knife in the other.

Gabe swung the pistol toward the charging Apache, using only instinct for his aim, and dropped the hammer and let the bullet fly. The pistol roared, bucked, and spat flame that illumined the snarling face of the wide-eyed screaming warrior. His hair hung straight below the wide hair band, his bare chest showed shiny sweat in the moonlight, his breech cloth gathered between flailing bare legs, and high-topped moccasins thudded on the gravelly ground. But the .54 caliber ball stopped his assault as it smashed into his face, jerking his head backwards and knocking him off his feet, as he fell to crash into the rocky ground flat of his back. His lips fluttered as he exhausted his last breath, his chest refusing to rise to take another.

Gabe dropped to one knee, keeping the rocks at his back, and searched the shadows for another attacker but nothing moved. The horses were fidgety, side stepping and looking around, and Gabe was unmoving. He frowned as he thought of the uncharacteristic behavior of Wolf who had disappeared in the trees and glanced side to side, hopeful of seeing his friend. Suddenly movement caught his eye, just past the horses, as a feathered lance sailed toward him. He threw himself to the side, rolling as he hit the ground and hearing the long lance clatter among the rocks. As he put his hand to the ground to rise, the scream of a charging warrior came from behind the horses and the warrior charged, his tomahawk raised for a killing blow. But a black shadow sailed overhead as Wolf used the rocks as his high ground launch. The big wolf's front paws and teeth found purchase on the screaming warrior who went down under the impact of the wolf. With a growl and a snarl, Wolf silenced the screams of the Apache, his teeth buried in the man's throat. Wide eyes lost their grip on life as the spirit of the Jicarilla renegade departed in the darkness. Wolf was astraddle the body when Gabe called, "Here boy, c'mere." Wolf turned his bloody maw toward his friend, glanced down at the remains of the warrior, and trotted to the side of Gabe.

Gabe knelt beside Wolf, running his hand through the big black's scruff, "Thanks boy." And as he looked from the wolf to the body of the mutilated warrior, he spoke softly, "So, now what? They gonna keep sending warriors back after us? And with none of 'em returning, then what?" He shook his head, looking around, listening, wondering if there were more, but Wolf sat easy and a glance at the horses showed they had settled down. "And are they gonna do somethin' to Ezra because of these? There just ain't no figgerin' on these Apache." He glanced at the stars, guessing it to be just past midnight then looked to the nearby hills. The sliver of moon and the stars did little to offer much light but he was comfortable in the darkness knowing there were always ways to see where there was nothing to be seen. He trusted the senses of Wolf and Ebony as well as his own, believing himself more than capable in the darkness, and the peril of his friend outweighed any hesitation or doubt that might arise. But he could only travel as fast and as far as the horses were able. *They've got to stop soon, their horses aren't any more capable than mine, and their tracks show several are already dragging their feet,* he thought as he mounted up and resumed the chase.

* * * * *

"*Ha'dishéí chíníí,* we must stop soon, the horses," suggested *Chish Kaaldi.* The speaker, Woodpecker, was speaking to the war chief of their band, Singing Dog.

"We will stop at the Nambe. There is water and grass for the horses," answered Singing Dog, snarling at Woodpecker. Dog was known as a surly man, friends with no one and a formidable enemy and proven fighter. This was the third outing for the band of renegade Jicarilla Apache, their band had separated themselves from the traditional village under the leadership of *Ba'i itso,* White Wolf, as their chief and Singing Dog as their war leader. The separation came when White Wolf had turned on a friendly village of the Mexicans and taken several young women as captives. When Wolf had been turned out for going against the word of the chief, *Vittorio,* it split the village with many choosing to go with White Wolf, for Wolf had made an agreement to trade all captives to the Lieutenant from the garrison at Santa Fe and the people of his band prospered.

Woodpecker looked at the war leader, moving up beside him, "The captive, he is not like others we have taken. Some are saying he is a Ga'an."

Singing Dog stopped and turned to scowl at Woodpecker, "A Ga'an?" he asked, incredulously.

"Yes. They say he is the last of the Ga'an, the one with the roaring club and is all black. This man is strong and black like the Ga'an."

"But the stick?"

"He has a big war club that would be a great stick that would roar like the Ga'an." In Apache custom, the Ga'an were mountain spirits, sent by Usen, the Creator, to teach the Apache to live in harmony with those around them. The first four dancers wore black head-coverings and masks and headdresses but the fifth was the protector that was sent to drive away evil spirits with the sound of his humming bull roarer, a great stick that he swung around his head and made a great noise to drive them away. He was a formidable spirit and all were afraid of him.

Dog frowned, looked back at the captive who was now sitting astride of his big bay horse led by a warrior. His hands were tied behind him and his feet were bound beneath the belly of the horse. He had been stripped of his buckskin shirt and now wore only the britches and moccasins. His broad shoulders and upper arm muscles glistened with sweat in the moonlight. Although his head hung, he still sat erect and was an impressive figure in the darkness.

Dog looked back at Woodpecker, growled, "He is just a black man, not a Ga'an! If he were a Ga'an, we could not bind him!"

"But the others have not returned. Some believe it is the power of the Ga'an." He paused, looking at Singing Dog, then asked, "Have you ever seen a black man like this before?"

Dog looked back at Woodpecker, his nostrils flaring and the muscles in his cheeks and neck rippling in anger, "He is not a Ga'an!" he declared and dug heels to his mount, moving quickly away from Woodpecker.

20 / DISSENSION

Ezra did not understand the tongue of the Jicarilla but there were certain words that were similar to what he knew of the Shoshone language and they often used words in Spanish. He picked up bits and pieces but the only thing he was certain of was that most of the warriors seemed to have a fear of him. He kept hearing the word, "Ga'an" as they gestured to him. And when they pulled him from the horse, they jumped back when he growled at them and struggled to his feet. At the command of their leader, four men grabbed him and pushed him to the ground, tying his hands to his feet behind his back, making it necessary to lie on his side or stomach. Fortunately, they had placed him on a pile of leaves at the foot of a tall cottonwood. Their camp was near a small stream and well concealed with the cottonwood, mesquite, and willows.

When two riderless horses walked into their camp in the early morning hours, the men were roused and caught the animals, chattering among themselves. Ezra recognized the horses as those ridden by the last two men sent to their backtrail by the leader of the raiders. One man appeared to confront the leader and argued as he gestured to the back trail and to Ezra. But Ezra pretended to still be asleep as the reflected light from the brilliant fiery red sunrise illumined the camp.

The leader stepped back from the others and started barking orders and gesturing to Ezra. Two men came to stand behind him, removing the cords they used to bind his hands to his feet. Ezra stretched out his legs, relieved to flex his muscles and rolled to his stomach to try to get to his feet, his hands still bound behind him. He drew his legs up under him and pushed away from the ground with his shoulder and came to his knees, then stood. He turned to face his captors, and the men stepped back, wide-eyed and pointing to Ezra's chest as they muttered to one another, stepping further away.

Ezra frowned, looked down at his chest and saw a jumble of crushed leaves stuck to his skin. He scowled, looking at the men as they shouted, "Ga'an!" while pointing at his chest. He looked down again and saw matted leaves stuck to his sweaty chest but only between his chest muscles and down to his navel as well as across his ribs below his larger chest muscles. He looked again, twisting around to try to see better, and to the men. Others had come near and were chattering to one another and gesturing to Ezra but Ezra stood staring back, a little perplexed. He saw the leader and another man walking towards him, talking to one another, and looking at him.

"It is the sign of the cross!" declared Woodpecker, pointing to the leaves on Ezra's chest. "It is like the sign used by the Ga'an!" The cross symbol was used by the masked Ga'an to signify the four directions and that evil comes from everywhere. To counter the evil, the Ga'an are the mountain spirits that can drive away the evil and protect the people. It is the Ga'an that teach the Apache to live in harmony. The greatest of the crown dancers of the mountain spirits is the fifth dancer or the clown dancer who is the only one that is black. This Ga'an uses his great stick or humming bull-roarer to protect the people.

"We have bound him and taken his great club and he cannot protect the people. That is why so many of our warriors have not returned!" declared Woodpecker, motioning to Ezra and harping on his belief to Singing Dog. The two came nearer, staring at the black man with the large muscles. His chest and shoulders rippled as he stood glaring at his captors and, even in the cool of the morning, his skin glistened with sweat. The black man turned his gaze on the war leader and his companion and growled as he narrowed his eyes and curled his lip.

"This is no Ga'an!" shouted Singing Dog. "Bind him and put him on his horse. We will sell him to the Lieutenant for a great price! Perhaps we can trade him for the soldier guns!"

The mention of the weapons of the soldiers brought everyone's attention to their leader. They looked from him to their captive and back again as he shouted, "Put him on his horse!" Two others joined the men standing nearest Ezra and they approached him cautiously but Ezra knew there was little he could do with his hands bound behind his back and being outnumbered by a dozen to one. He stood, lifting his head proudly, and turned toward his big bay. He watched while one of the men saddled the horse and stepped near to climb aboard. Two men held his arms as he raised his foot to the stirrup, then lifted him up to swing his leg over the saddle. He glanced to his right pants leg, reassuring himself of the scabbarded knife that was hidden in the high top of his moccasin and covered by his pants leg. But one knife was little comfort.

* * * * *

"This report," began the Alcalde, Juan Bautista de Anza, also called the governor, "tells of an Apache raid on the Escalante Hacienda north of Santa Cruz.

You take the second platoon, a week's rations and track down these renegades!" He barked the orders to Lieutenant Manuel Delgado who stood with First Sergeant Juan de Abrego at his side.

The Lieutenant asked, "When did the report say the attack happened?"

"It did not say, just that the report was sent as soon as they heard!" growled the Alcalde. "You must not waste time!" he snarled. His disdain for this man was obvious but there was no other officer available for the assignment. "Well?"

The lieutenant snapped a crisp salute, as did the Sergeant, and replied, "Yes sir!" When the salute was returned, although a bit lazily by the Alcalde, the men turned on their heels and exited the room. As they walked from the rear door of the governor's palace, the Sergeant glanced at the Lieutenant, "You knew this would come, didn't you sir?"

"Yes. That is why I sent word to Singing Dog about the Negra and his friend. He will bring a handsome price from the Comancheros!" he laughed, nodding to the First Sergeant. The Sergeant laughed and summoned Sergeant Ygnacio Duran, "Assemble the second platoon! One week's rations and ammunition!"

"Si, mi sergeant!" answered the subordinate turning to his assigned task.

Within the half hour, the platoon of ten Soldados de Cuera, two corporals, two sergeants and the lieutenant, left the garrison to follow the well-used trail to the north, the same trail initially taken by Gabe and Ezra the day before. The men were outfitted in their leather armor, halberds, and the standard issue M1757 Musket Miquelet lock rifle.

It was mid-afternoon when the scout, Phelipe Rodriquez, returned to the formation of soldados. He saluted the Lieutenant and reported, "Sir, there where the buzzards are circling, three bodies, Apache!"

"How long ago?" asked the Lieutenant.

"One day, maybe less. The varmints have been at them for some time, it is hard to tell."

"What about the Americans?"

"No sign sir, that I could tell. There were many tracks, but the coyotes, buzzards, and more . . ." he shrugged as he cocked his head to the side.

Lieutenant Delgado waved the man away, sending him back to scout. He shook his head as he looked at the First Sergeant, "We will follow the tracks of the Americans!"

"But Lieutenant, our orders are to go to Santa Cruz and on to the Escalante Hacienda. We are to find the Apache renegades!"

"Si, but I believe the renegades are to the north. Were not these Apache," motioning to the circling buzzards, "a part of the renegades?"

"Si, Lieutenant," answered the First Sergeant, grinning at the wily leader of the foray.

"And is not our friend, Singing Dog, the leader of these renegades?"

"Si, Lieutenant."

"Then we are on the right trail, are we not?" grinned the officer.

The first Sergeant nodded, grinning, and turned back to the men to relay the Lieutenant's orders. Yet he also believed the officer was right in his assumption that these Apache were the same as the renegades that assaulted the hacienda, and if so, they would probably find more evidence of the raiding renegades, perhaps even the remains of the American.

21 / TRAIL

Another two, almost three hours of moving slowly across the perilous and dark terrain brought Gabe to another green-bottomed arroyo. They moved off the north-facing slope to drop into the bottom, trees and brush showing black in the dim light. The whisper of hooves told of a sandy bottom, but the smell of fresh water was in the air and they pushed into the thickets. Gabe paused, listening, and the faint sound of gurgling water told of either a trickle of a creek or a nearby spring. He gave Ebony his head and let the horse push through some more willows to take them to the water.

After letting the horses have their drink, Gabe and Wolf put their faces in the little pool and drank deeply. Gabe sat back on his heels, looking around in the deep shadows, and stood to move back from the brush and have a better view of the arroyo. He saw the trail at the edge of the long sloping bank and sauntered near to examine the tracks. They had been following the trail of the Apache, always watching for any more sign of warriors splitting off to watch their back trail but, since the last two, there had been no more.

With a glance to the remaining stars, Gabe decided to take cover in the trees, let the horses get some rest, and hopefully get at least a couple of hours of sleep himself. He stripped the gear from the animals, gave them a good rub down with handfuls of grass, then picketed them within reach of the water and graze. Rolling his blanket under the overreaching branches of a big mesquite, he lay down with Wolf at his side and was soon asleep.

It was Wolf's cold nose on his neck that brought him instantly awake, his pistol in his hand as he sat up. The first light of morning had given the sky a grey tint and all was quiet. He looked at Wolf who stood at his side, looking toward the horses. A quick glance showed no alarm and Gabe came to his feet as he searched the edges of the brush and trees between their camp and the trail. There was no movement nor sound and Gabe, frowning, looked at Wolf who still stood facing the horses. Gabe looked their direction again, then back at Wolf and paused, something was different.

He slowly turned toward the horses and saw three

tails swishing at the early morning mites and flies and realized, there were three. He frowned and stuffed the pistol in his belt as he walked closer, recognizing the rump of the bay mule and as he looked he saw the pack, still secure aboard the beast. He shook his head and walked closer, moving beside the mule, putting his hand on his neck, and speaking softly to him, "Where you been, boy? And how'd you find us?" There were several brambles in the tail of the mule, the packs and panniers were a little askew, but still secure, and the mule turned to look at Gabe as if to say, "Why didn't you wait?"

Gabe shook his head and began stripping the gear from the mule. He stacked the packs and panniers aside and grabbed up a handful of grass and began rubbing him down. Dried lather flaked white, wet hair stood when brushed with the grass, but the mule was enjoying the rubdown. Gabe noticed a couple of spots by the withers and one where the breeching passed under the tail that were showing a little wear and in need of care. Gabe finished the rubdown and left the trees for a patch of agave, cut a big spine, and returned to the mule. He applied the sap from the agave to the spots and chose to give the animals a little more rest while he had something to eat but first he wanted to get his scope and have a look see, maybe find the Apache.

With a wave to Wolf, he instructed, "You stay

here with the horses, boy, watch out for 'em!" and started up the steep slope to the mesa top. The sun was painting the bellies of the low-lying clouds with a brilliant fiery red that faded to gold, casting a glow upon the many flat-top mesas around the arroyo, as Gabe took a seat beside a clump of sage, enough to shield him from any watchers. To his right were the higher timbered mountains, one or two that stuck their granite peaks above timberline. To the west, miles, and miles of rolling high desert, freckled with juniper and piñon. And to the north, more of the same, rolling hills, flat-top mesas, long ridges, and endless ravines, gullies, and arroyos. Yet far to the north, the faint shadows of distant peaks beckoned him home. As he unlimbered the telescope, he prayed, "Lord, you know the fix we're in; Ezra's a captive of some blood-thirsty Apache and there's a sight more of them than just me'n Wolf. I guess I'm askin' ya' Lord, to keep him safe and guide me to him 'fore it's too late. I sure don't want to go back to Dove and his young'uns without him. Now, Lord, you know I ain't itchin' to get in a fight and I ain't a hankerin' to go shootin' and killin' anybody but if that's what I've got to do to get my brother back from the devil's horde, then so be it. In the meantime, I'd sure appreciate it if you could watch over our families till we get home. Thank you, Lord." He breathed deep, his shoulders lifting as he shook his head, then finished with, "Let your will be done. In Jesus' name, Amen."

He stretched out the telescope and began his scan. To the northwest, he saw a green bottomed valley that was fed by three streams including the one where he camped. He saw what he thought were houses but movement nearer caught his attention. Crossing the confluence of two of the feeder creeks were several riders, *Apache!* In the middle of the line of riders, Gabe recognized the dark image of his shirtless friend, *He's alive!* thought Gabe, trying to focus in on the figure, but the riders disappeared into a ravine. Gabe watched a moment longer, then rose and started down the slope, bounding and digging in his heels, making great leaping strides to get to the horses. No longer concerned that someone would see or hear him, he hurriedly saddled and rigged the horses and mule, checked the loads in his weapons, and as an afterthought, slipped the Mongol bow from its case and sat down to string his favorite weapon. He hung the bow on the pommel and swung aboard, thinking all the while about his route and approach. If he did it right, he should be able to overtake them around mid-day but what he would do then would be dictated by the terrain and position of the captors.

Ezra did his best to be observant without giving his captors the idea he was watching. His eyes were on the surly leader, the man that ruled with force and anger; his men feared him but showed little respect for him. It was the leader who had commandeered his weapons and war club and had hung the powder horn and possibles bag over his shoulders in the same way he had seen Ezra carry them but Ezra got the impression the man did not know how to use them. He had also noticed Singing Dog favoring his wounded leg, the wide bandage showing blood. Ezra took a little satisfaction in knowing the wound was from Gabe's arrow at their first encounter after their raid on the hacienda. Singing Dog rode with the rifle, wrapped in Ezra's tunic like a sheath, across the withers of his horse, the pistol stuffed in his breechcloth, and the war club lay across the back of the horse just behind the man, secured by the same cord used to bind Ezra.

The band crossed a confluence of two creeks and Ezra looked downstream to see the wider valley showing green and a quick glimpse of an adobe structure, probably a farmer's home. They moved into a dry ravine, climbed the low bank, and started north, bearing a little to the west. When Singing Dog and Woodpecker dropped off a slight rise, they turned to the north on a good trail that pointed towards the distant hills that appeared to rise from the flats with ridges that slashed white with rimrock. Ezra guessed the hills to be about seven or eight miles away and the sun was already beating down on their shoulders and backs, sapping moisture and strength from both man and beast. He looked at the warriors who showed little discomfort, their only attire being the headband that held the long hair away from their faces, breechcloths, and high-topped moccasins. Unlike other plains tribes, the Apache did not use feathers or beading, did not braid their hair and had little use for leggings or tunics.

Across the flats, the band rode side by side, separated but clustered together; although no one spoke, but everyone was watchful. Ezra's skin glistened with sweat, he felt the trickle of perspiration down his back and chest, tasted it on his lips and wiped his brow, his bound hands coming away wet. They had failed to tie his feet together like before and his hands were now bound before him, the end of the cord wrapped around the saddle horn, but with enough slack for him to move. He thought about the knife in his moccasin, flexed his knees and knew he could, if necessary, lift his leg to the pommel and across the withers and be able to reach the knife and cut his bonds, but with no weapon and outnumbered a dozen to one, it would not be a smart move. Best wait for a better opportunity.

The return of a scout caused Singing Dog to rein up and wait for his word. As the man came near, he spoke in low tones, motioning behind him, nodding and grinning. When they started again, it was at a canter until they broke over a rise that opened into a wide cut between two ridges that rose a couple hundred feet on either side. Before them was a green bottomed valley and Singing Dog pulled to a stop, holding his hand up for the others to come near. As they gathered close, he spoke and gestured to the valley. Ezra saw two adobe structures with other outbuildings, probably Mexican ranchos. When he saw Singing Dog motioning toward the structures and speaking to his men, he realized they were about to attack the people in the field and homes and he was unable to warn them or help them.

The band separated into two groups, one led by Singing Dog, the other led by Woodpecker. With a warrior on either side of him, one taking the rein of Ezra's bay and wrapping it around his hand, they followed the two groups until the leader's group went to the left around the point of the ridge that pushed into the valley and the second group, led by Woodpecker, rode straight north across the little creek that fed the valley. Once through the willows and brush, the two warriors with Ezra kept to the flank of the steep-sided hill on the east edge of the valley while Woodpecker's group started into the valley toward the adobe huts.

As Ezra watched, the second group sided the trees and brush on the creek bank and the first group started across the fields below the houses. At an unseen sign from Singing Dog, both groups started toward the houses at a full gallop. As they neared, the war cries filled the valley, but Ezra's captors kicked their horses into a canter to round the end of the hills and take to the mesas on the north side of the valley. All Ezra knew of the attack was the fading screams of war cries and frightened women. He shook his head as his mount was led close to the side of one of the men and followed by the other. He gritted his teeth as anger flared. He thought of the helpless farmers' families and hoped there were no children.

22 / CAPTIVES

It was the kind of country that could hide a raiding party of a hundred warriors but, at the same time, show a solitary rider from five miles away. With the rolling hills, scattered trees, clumps of sage taller than a man, and innumerable ravines and gullies, Gabe stayed hidden from the Apache. He knew predators seldom saw themselves as prey nor the hunter considered themselves the hunted and it was that mindset that Gabe would use against them. He also noted their manner of travel was more direct instead of using the contours of the country to make it easy on the horses and the direct route often left the usual trail to traverse the ridges and hills. Gabe wondered if they had an objective in mind for another raid, perhaps a small settlement or single hacienda like the first.

Gabe chose to use the trail and easier route to spare the horses but would make it up by the pace.

Ebony was eager to stretch out and willingly took to the canter. With the grey usually traveling free rein, Gabe tied the mule's lead line to the pack saddle of the grey and glanced back to see them keeping pace with the black, less than half a length behind. He stood in his stirrups to look ahead and quickly spotted the dust of the bigger band of Apache. With the dry country and no wind, it was impossible for that many riders to move without kicking up a considerable dust cloud. But a band that size would be unconcerned about being seen, and with the typical arrogant leader, they would assume themselves invulnerable.

He spotted a bit of a ridge that rose about a hundred feet above the flats, reined Ebony to a walk and moved behind the ridge. He slipped down, scope in hand and quickly mounted the ridge. As he reached the crest, he bellied down and stretched out the scope. He centered it on the dust cloud just in time to see the band crest a saddle between two higher ridges and drop to the other side. Beyond the cut, he saw the glimmer of green, recognizing it to be a fertile valley below. He frowned, rose, and slid down the slope to the horses, thinking about the raiders and trying to guess what they were doing.

Without delay, he mounted up and took to the trail, believing the Apache to be out of sight, making him out of their sight. He kicked the black to a ground-eating canter, the grey and mule, determined not to be left behind, kept pace with the stallion. As he neared the cut between the ridges and the saddle crossing, he slowed and walked the black slowly toward the crest. Before exposing himself, he stopped, stood in his stirrups to look ahead, and nudged the horse forward a couple steps, then more, until he saw the raiders in the lower end of the cut, just breaking into the open of the green valley. It was then he spotted the buildings and knew immediately what was planned.

He slipped the scope from the case and lifted it to his eye to watch the movements of the Apache. They split into two groups and Gabe spotted the figure of Ezra. His scope followed that group as they crossed the creek and he saw the two men with Ezra break off to move alongside the flank of the big hill. Gabe glanced around quickly, slid down and ground tied the black and ran and climbed up the side of the ridge to the right. Once atop, he gasped for air and searched for the riders with Ezra. They were gone.

He quickly scanned the terrain around the big hill, looking for a way to circle around and hopefully catch Ezra and his captors. *There!* he whispered as he saw a dry gulch that appeared to offer a way around the hill and maybe intercept the others. Without hesitation, he bounded down the slope and swung aboard the black. With a quick slap of his legs, he said, "Let's go boy!" He took the same trail toward the valley as was taken by the Apache but, once at the bottom, he turned the black to the right toward a cut behind the big hill and to the dry gulch. They stretched out, unconcerned about the Apache who were busy with their attack, and quickly rounded the end of the hill and took to the sandy-bottomed ravine. As he thought, within a short distance, the dry gulley sided the butte and, in less than a mile, he spotted the narrow arroyo with the feeder creek. He was certain this was the way the two Apache had brought Ezra.

As he neared the arroyo, he slowed, standing in his stirrups for a quick look, then nudged Ebony into the grassy banks beside the creek bottom. With a glance, he could see this was nothing but a feeder draw and would only have water after a rainstorm or with spring runoff. He looked for the tracks and quickly spotted the trail on the far side of the creek. He looked down at Wolf, "Go! Find Ezra!" and the black wolf took off at a run. As Gabe started to dig heels to Ebony, the big stallion lunged to the chase and Gabe had to grab leather to stay with him. A quick glance showed the grey and the mule were close behind.

The thunder of hooves behind them caused the two warriors to turn around and the sight of several horses charging after them was enough but to see a big black wolf, ears laid back and growling and snapping as he ran struck them with fear like a lightning bolt. Both men kicked their horses to a run, the one without the rein lunging into the lead, the other jerking and pulling at the rein of the bay with Ezra aboard. He turned toward Ezra just in time to see the big wolf seemingly bounce off the wall of the canyon and come flying through the air straight at him, teeth bared. The warrior screamed, dropped the rein and lifted his arm to protect his face only to have the wolf knock him from his horse and bear him to the ground, teeth buried in his arm. The man hit the hard trail on his back, frantically trying to push the wolf off, but his flailing arms exposed his throat and Wolf bit and ripped, tearing the man's throat away, muffling his death rattle.

Gabe brought Ebony to a stop and jumped to the ground, an arrow in one hand, the bow in the other. He watched the first warrior fleeing but nocked the arrow and quickly brought the bow to full draw, drew his bead and sent the feathered shaft whistling in pursuit of its prey. The warrior arched his back as the arrow was buried next to his spine, and slowly tumbled to the side, bouncing end over end and stopping in a twisted jumble as the horse continued its running escape.

When he saw Wolf coming at a run, Ezra lifted his leg across the pommel, lifted his leggings and grabbed his knife from the scabbard. With one quick slash, he cut his bonds and reached for the rein but the warrior had dropped the rein and was fighting with wolf. Ezra leaned over the neck of the bay, and picked up the rein, bringing the bay to a stop as he watched Wolf finish off the Apache. He glanced to his left to see Gabe dismount and take aim with the bow and watched as the other Apache tumbled to the ground. He looked over at his friend, "Those others will be coming along soon, we might wanna make ourselves a little scarce!"

Gabe chuckled, hung the bow on the pommel and swung aboard, "Sounds reasonable! Follow me!"

Gabe led them on the hard-packed trail that crossed the narrow gulch and followed a high ridge into the hills beyond. When he spotted a break in the terrain, he turned the horses into the cut and moved into a narrow draw thick with trees. On either side, a tall ridge afforded a good view of their back trail and the surrounding terrain. He slipped down, motioned to the saddle, "I'm goin' up there. If you need 'em, the rifle's in the scabbard and the pistols are in the holsters. I'll be right back!"

He quickly climbed the ridge, stood between two piñons, and turned to search their back trail and more. As he watched, he saw movement and spotted some of the warriors riding the same trail they did through the narrow arroyo. Behind them were more and as he counted, he numbered thirteen riders. He focused in on those in the lead and recognized two riders to be young women, bound and wearing tattered clothes, faces wet with tears and eyes full of fear.

The leader stopped, looking around, and slipped to the ground, and another warrior sided him. Gabe grinned as he saw them looking at the body of the first warrior. *Wonder what they're thinkin' since he was killed by Wolf!* The men had gone to one knee, touching the ground and Gabe knew they were looking at the tracks of the wolf and chuckled. One man jumped to his feet, searching the surrounding hillsides, and shouted something to those behind him prompting a jittery response as they also looked around, fearfully.

The first two mounted up and slowly moved up the draw, drawing closer to the wider bosque where the trails split, still nervously searching the countryside. When they spotted the second warrior, the same two dismounted, and one picked up the broken shaft of the black arrow and looked around, more frantic than before. Gabe saw the bandage on the man's leg and chuckled as he knew this man had recognized the arrow to be the same as the one that had taken him in the leg. The man quickly mounted, shouted to his men, and turned to take the trail that would lead them north into the hills and away from Gabe and Ezra. Gabe nodded and went below to join his friend.

23 / OBSERVATION

"They've headed north. I think findin' the first body done in by Wolf and the second with a black arrow mighta spooked their leader," shared Gabe as he stepped into the cluster of trees. Ezra stood looking through the copse, rifle in hand, and turned to face his friend.

"Yeah, that leader, whatever his name is, is a wretched butcher! He's got my weapons and shirt and I aim to get 'em back!" growled Ezra, standing before his friend.

"Well, now he's got a couple Mexican farm girls!"

"Then what're we gonna do?" asked Ezra, knowing his friend would not stand by and not do everything he could to rescue the girls.

"Reckon the first step is to follow 'em," drawled Gabe, slipping the rein from the branch and sticking his foot in the stirrup to swing aboard.

"Where'd they go?"

"Took off to the northwest, headin' to that long ridge yonder," stated Gabe, pointing to the sparsely timbered ridge that stretched out from the higher eastern mountains into the wide desert plains on the west. "That's their dust cloud, there," he nodded to the wispy pale dust cloud at the base of the ridge. "We'll be outta their sight in that arroyo and can get closer to 'em. Once we crest that ridge, we'll have a better idea where they're goin'."

Ezra nudged the bay alongside Ebony and asked, "What'chu got to eat?"

Gabe turned to look at his friend, shook his head and reached back into the saddlebags and produced a handful of pemmican for Ezra, "That's the last of the pemmican, so enjoy!" suggested Gabe, grinning at his always hungry friend.

"Hey, those boys didn't feed me at all and I'm hungry! After all, I'm still a growin' boy!"

"Yeah, you're growin' alright, *around!*" laughed Gabe. He reined up, stood in his stirrups as he looked to the distant ridge, then brought out his scope. He stretched out the brass telescope and focused it on the point where the raiders had crossed and searched the long ridge. "There doesn't appear to be any left to watch their backtrail. Wherever they're goin', they must be in a hurry."

"Near as I could gather, they're just goin' to their

camp, then they'll be wantin' to meet up with the Comancheros to sell those girls. I'm purty sure that's what they were goin' to do with me, but they kept usin' the word, Lieutenant. You don't suppose he had somethin' to do with all this, do you?"

Gabe frowned as he looked back to Ezra, feasting on the pemmican, and asked, "You sure they were sayin' Lieutenant?"

"Ummhmmm, that's one of the few words I understood. That and Comanchero. I did hear the leader say somethin' 'bout the soldier guns. He slapped my rifle when he did and the others got excited about it."

Gabe remembered their first encounter with the Lieutenant at the Garrison in Santa Fe. He had been determined to take Ezra as a prisoner solely because of his being a black man and assumed to be an escaped slave. If Pedro Vial had not intervened, the situation could have turned ugly and the Lieutenant backed down too quickly and was obviously not pleased. Gabe frowned as he took a last look at the ridge and re-cased the scope. He slowly shook his head as he thought about the Lieutenant. He had known men that were willing to walk on the wrong side of the law and where there was no law to make up their own, all in the name of money. He glanced at Ezra, thinking, as the Lieutenant might have, and knew a man of Ezra's build and stature would command a hefty price in the slave trade but any slave market was a long way from Santa Fe. And was the Lieutenant the prospective buyer for the young women? According to what Vial had explained, the buying and selling of captives was a common practice in this land. The Apache and Navajo would steal women and youngsters from the Mexicans and sell them to the Comancheros who would return them to the settlers for a price. And the Mexicans and others would take them from Navajo and the Apache and sell them to other Mexicans or to the Comancheros who would sell them to the Comanches. *So, if we get the young women back from the Apache, then what?* wondered Gabe.

As they crested the long ridge, they reined up and stepped down. The juniper and piñon were thicker here and the land was scarred with many ravines and gulches. Before them, the tracks of the Apache were evident, the dry sandy soil was turned with the tracks of over a dozen horses. Gabe stretched out the scope as Ezra pointed, "Say, ain't that the long mesa that stood above that first hacienda the Apache hit? It was on the other side," he paused as he looked, then pointed, "bout there or so."

As Gabe scanned the area, he saw the green at the base of the long mesa, followed it to the westernmost point and recognized that area as the confluence of the Rio Grande and Chama rivers. "I believe you're right, Ezra. But the Apache went thataway!" he nodded toward the eastern half of the long mesa. "I'm thinkin' their camp is in the bosque by the river at the base there."

Gabe glanced up at the sun that was lowering toward the long mesa, "And they will probably make camp before dark."

"Think we could get there before dark so we could see where the girls are?" asked Ezra, shading his eyes as he strained to see in the distance.

"Prob'ly, but we'll have to take it easy the closer we get. There's usually some high banks along the river that might give us a view from far enough away that we won't be seen."

"And that's what, eight, ten miles?" asked Ezra, nodding toward the mesa.

"Yeah, 'bout that."

Ezra looked at the sun, then to Gabe, "We can make that - easy!"

Gabe nodded, "As long as the Apache don't have other ideas," and stuffed the scope back in the case and stepped aboard the black. With a wave of his hand, he sent Wolf to scout the trail before them and a squeeze of his knees started Ebony down toward the trail taken by the Apache.

The meandering trail followed the sandy-bottomed draw, taking the easiest way as run-off water always did, and soon merged with another dry wash that came from the eastern mountains. Less than a mile later, the tracks of the Apache left the draw to climb the low slope and cross a low ridge to the north. With Wolf in the lead, Gabe and Ezra followed, staying on the tracks of the Apache. The trail meandered a short ways, always pointing to the northwest, until it broke into a wider gulch that had carried a much larger run-off, but now lay bottomed with dry sandy soil, the only remains of early spring run-off.

The tracks of the Apache, showing freshly turned soil and evidence it had been less than a half hour since they passed, followed the dry wash toward the green bottomed valley that lay in the shadow of the long mesa that stood above the Rio Grande. Gabe reined up, looking down the draw, and scanning the nearby ridges as he turned to look at Ezra. "I think we're gettin' mighty close to their camp. The river valley is just down there," nodding to the western mouth of the wash, "and I'm thinkin' that's where they're headed." He looked around, then nodded to the north of the draw at another ridge, "What say we cross over there, then move toward the river. That way we won't be comin' out the same place they did, cuz if they thought somebody was followin', that's where they'd be watchin'."

"Sounds reasonable," nodded Ezra, motioning for Gabe to lead off. With a wave to Wolf to come alongside, they left the trail and started through the scattered trees and sage to the indicated ridge. Wolf dropped onto an easy game trail and followed it to the crest but stopped before the peak and turned to Gabe. With a nod and a grin, Gabe stepped down, scope in hand and slowly moved to the crest and with the scope outstretched, made a quick survey. Nothing showed nor moved except a dust devil that danced down the draw, lifted, and disappeared. He glanced to Ezra, "It's clear, for a little way."

Before Gabe had mounted, Ezra pushed ahead to take the lead. The big bay mounted the ridge and stepped over the crest, then at Ezra's urging, took to the same trail that Wolf followed to descend into the wide dry bottomed valley. He watched the long high ridge that separated them from the bosque of the Rio Grande and, after less than two miles, the ridge sloped to a point, but Ezra pulled up, motioning to the mouth of the valley, spoke softly, "I'm guessin' that's where we get mighty near to the river. You wanna climb up there," motioning to the tapered off end of the ridge, "and look around?"

Gabe nodded, grabbed his scope, and slid to the ground, tossing the reins to Ezra and quickly climbed the ridge by utilizing a rounded shoulder that made a cut at the top. As he approached, he dropped to a crouch, looking beyond the ridge to the green bottomed valley, and the smell of smoke dropped him to his belly. He slowly moved closer to the crest, stretched out the scope and began a quick survey of the village directly below the ridge.

He counted fifteen wickiups, brush huts that housed the families of the warriors. To the far left, most of the villagers had gathered, probably for the return of the warriors. There was considerable chatter and movement, and as Gabe watched some young men led the horses of the returning warriors away from the village to a grassy meadow just downstream. Smaller groups were moving about the camp, animatedly talking, and moving, many gathering around cookfires and others going to their lodges. Gabe searched for the two captives, finally spotting them being led with cords around their necks, their hands tied behind them, and women with fresh-cut switches whipping them as they struggled to keep up with their captors. They were led to a wickiup at the edge of the camp near the river, pushed inside and followed by two women. The men turned away and left, apparently going to their own lodges. The women soon exited, chattering to one another, and went to different wickiups. Nothing moved near the lodge where the girls had been placed. Gabe marked it in his mind, looking at the rest of the camp, the lay of the land around the camp, and the possible access to the brush hut. Satisfied, he crabbed back away from the ridge to return to Ezra. As he stepped and slid down the slope, he watched his footing, doing his best to leave no sign of his passing, paused, and looked across the draw for a possible campsite, and satisfied, was soon at Ezra's side.

24 / PREPARING

"The village is just over this ridge, maybe fifteen lodges, brush huts," stated Gabe as he started to mount Ebony.

"Did you see the girls?" asked Ezra.

"Yeah, they're in a lodge near the river. Might be easy to get to," answered Gabe, leaning his forearms on the pommel, looking at Ezra.

"Did you see which one was the leader's?"

"Uh, no, wasn't lookin' for him."

"Gimme the scope!" demanded Ezra, "I need to know where he is so I can get my weapons and tunic back!" Gabe raised his eyebrows as he looked at the determined expression of Ezra and handed off the scope.

"I'll go up that draw behind me and make a camp."

Ezra nodded and swung the bay around to take to the trees at the base of the ridge. The sun was beginning to paint the bellies of the few remaining clouds, back lighting the long flat-top mesa beyond the river and stretching long shadows toward the camp of the Apache. Ezra bellied down and stretched out the scope and began his scan of the many wickiups, searching for any giveaway that would tell of the lodge of Singing Dog. The village lay at the mouth of a long canyon cut by the Rio Grande, the roaring rapids rumbling in the deep maw of the gorge. As the river broke into the narrow end of the valley, the camp of the Apache was at a juncture of three fingers of land. The westernmost on the far side of the river was a finger ridge that fell from the long mesa and jutted into the river bed, moving the river around its point. To the north was a high rising black mesa, its shoulder pushing the river into a narrow and deep channel. Between the black mesa and the ridge where Ezra lay, was the mouth of a long arroyo that sided the black mesa, and its alluvial fan offered a sandy shore on the east bank of the river. It was just below this three-point junction where the many wickiups were scattered.

Ezra searched the encampment, noting several lodges had horses tethered nearby, a practice of most native people to keep their favorite war horse at hand. The animals would be hand fed, led to water often, and groomed by the rider, ensuring the bond between man and horse. He remembered the distinctive black and white piebald ridden by Singing Dog but did not see it among the lodges until, near the lodge closest to the ridge, the big horse stepped from behind the wickiup. Ezra grinned when he saw the tethered animal and Singing Dog beside him, rubbing him down with a piece of blanket.

Ezra scanned the lodge and its location as it sat near the ridge, slightly away from and higher than the other lodges. *Just like that arrogant jackanape, thinks he's higher and better than the others. Well, we'll just see about that!* whispered Ezra as he watched the camp. He scanned the rest of the camp, spotted what Gabe had described as the lodge that kept the girls, and with another quick scan, crabbed back from the ridge and returned to his horse to ride to the camp with Gabe.

He stepped down, started stripping the bay of his saddle and tack and after rubbing him down, tethered him in the trees beside the others. Returning to the makeshift camp with the stacked gear, he sat down opposite Gabe and accepted some strips of smoked meat as Gabe asked, "Find it?"

"Yeah. It's the one closest to the ridge here," nodding across the arroyo, "set back a little and above the others on a bit of a shoulder. I spotted his piebald and then saw him with the horse. So, I reckon my gear is in his wickiup. Didn't see no woman but prob'ly has one."

"You spot the one I said had the girls?"

"Yeah. You got any idea how we're gonna do this?" asked Ezra, munching on a piece of meat.

"Not sure, you?"

"I'm thinkin' I could hit the leader's hut, make a bit of a diversion and you could get the girls."

"Hittin' 'em ain't the problem, it's the gettin' away I'm concerned about!" declared Gabe, leaning forward, elbows on his knees as he looked at Ezra.

"Well, let's ponder on it a spell." He looked around, "I could think better if I had some coffee; ain't had none for a couple days and muh belly's tellin' me 'bout it."

Gabe shook his head, "Oh, we could fix some coffee alright but could we have it drunk before we got scalped?"

"There ya go, always ruinin' my wishin'!" drawled Ezra, grinning at his friend.

Gabe glanced at the sky, dusk was dropping its curtain and the colors had faded from the heavens. He pictured what he remembered of the encampment, thinking about their approach and escape routes. It was obvious they could not hit the upper end of the camp and escape downriver or could they? If they tried to return up the arroyo where they approached, the sandy bottom would make a fast escape difficult but also hinder anyone chasing them and the arroyo would be in the dark with the high ridges to the east and west. They would also need horses for the girls but that was only if it would be easily done. Without horses, they could ride double with them or put them on the packhorse and mule.

Gabe scowled, thinking, looked at Ezra, "What if we . . ." and began to detail his plan. Ezra leaned forward, listening, nodding, adding a thought, and the excitement grew as the plan took shape. When he was finished, Gabe leaned back, "What do you think? Think it'll work?" he asked, cocking his head to the side, and considering all they discussed.

"Sounds like it but, we both know, things don't always go as planned. Maybe we should have a secondary plan, you know, just in case."

"I think we'll just have to take it as it comes and think and act fast. After all, there's just two of us and how many of them?"

Ezra chuckled, "There were about a dozen that came back with the girls and probably that many in the encampment, not to mention the women and youngsters, both of which can be mighty mean!"

Gabe shook his head, "We've done some crazy things in our time but this one, well, might be the dumbest!"

Ezra let a slow grin split his face, then leaned back with an arm behind his head, "I'm gonna get some rest."

Gabe chuckled, "Guess I should too," and duplicated Ezra's moves and lay back beside Wolf.

When he slowly opened his eyes, he saw a clear night bedecked with brilliant stars. The moon was waxing toward full and showed about half but it was bright and offered ample light for their plan. Gabe judged it to be just after midnight as he listened to the cry of the nighthawk accompanied by the cicadas. The distant howl of a desert wolf got Wolf's attention as he came to his feet and listened. Below them came the squeal of a rabbit that had probably fallen prey to a prowling coyote or bobcat. Ezra slowly rose from his slumber, looking and listening, and without a word, went to the horses to start saddling.

Neither man spoke, yet each one knew the other was taking the time to talk to their God. Prayer had always been a part of their lives and they seldom attempted any challenge without taking the time to talk to their Savior. They quietly saddled the horses, loaded the packs and panniers on the packsaddles aboard the grey and the mule, then looked at one another. Gabe reached to his saddle and slipped one of the saddle pistols from the holster and handed it to Ezra. "If you need to reload, you'll have to find your horn and pouch to do it!"

"Plannin' on it." He hefted the big saddle pistol with its thirteen-inch over/under barrels and double locks, shook his head and added, "Almost have to have a horse to pack this thing!" and jammed it into his waistband. He walked ahead, leading the bay and the mule until they were in the bottom of the arroyo. He watched as Gabe mounted up, then handed him the reins to the bay. "You might wanna put the girls on the bay here and I'll see if I can snag a horse after I hit the leader's wickiup. Might even take his!" he declared, grinning. With a wave and a nod, he trotted across the arroyo and started up the slope of the ridge. A quick glance back showed Gabe starting down to the arroyo to the upper end of the encampment.

Ezra dug in his toes as he climbed the steep ridge and once atop, quickly started down the other side. He angled across the face of the slope, cautiously moving from tree to tree or clump of sage, moving as quietly as possible. Both he and Gabe had learned to move as quiet as the best of the natives and could easily make his way into the camp unheard and unseen. But anything could happen and usually does.

25 / ASSAULT

Ezra crouched beside a scraggly piñon, searching the encampment below the ridge. He started to move but the sudden sensation of icy fingers crawling up his back, stopped him. His innate ability to sometimes see and even foresee happenings because of his Celtic/Druid senses inherited from his mother had stopped him before and he paid close attention now. Without moving a muscle, he searched the terrain before him. The moonlight stretched shadows beside the trees and shrubbery but movement caught his attention. There, on the peak of the ridge above the camp, stood a lone watchman, what some tribes called dog soldiers. The man sat on an outcropping that extended from a formation of rimrock. Ezra breathed easy, relieved he was not watching the arroyo on the far side where Gabe was moving with the horses.

Ezra looked around, knowing he could not enter the camp without being seen by the lookout and knew he must first eliminate that threat. He moved just his eyes, searching for a route to the man's promontory, a route that would give him sufficient cover. He watched the man, saw him stand and stretch and take a step away toward the far side of the rimrock. Ezra quickly stepped away from the piñon, backtracking and moving uphill. He turned beside a thick clump of scrub oak and dropped to one knee, looking for the man. He had returned to his seat and now leaned back against the rocks.

Using the rocks to shield him, Ezra slowly crept closer, his movements so slow he watched a lizard pass him by without looking at him. He kept moving, keeping his eyes away from the man, knowing that a continual stare can alert even the less than wary. The senses of man are such that they can detect when someone is staring at them and he intentionally avoided the man, but kept moving, using only his peripheral vision to detect any movement. As he neared the rocks, he was behind and slightly above the man and leaned forward for a better look. As he expected, the man's breathing was easy and regular, his arms lay at his sides, his lance beside his hand, but not clasped.

Ezra grinned, knowing the man had fallen asleep but he also knew it was not a deep sleep and the slightest disturbance would awaken him. Ezra picked his next steps carefully, knowing each one had to be sure and solid. He slipped the pistol from his belt, took a firm grip, and quickly made the last three steps as silently as the others. He used the pistol as a club and brought the heavy barrels down on the back of the man's neck, quickly rendering him unconscious. Ezra grabbed him before he fell forward, leaned him back against the rocks and lay his lance across his lap. Anyone looking from below would see him at his post with his lance in hand. As he started to step away, he glanced at the man and saw no movement of his chest. A thin trickle of blood came from his mouth and his eyes were open but unmoving. Ezra knew the man was dead. He shook his head, *Musta hit him harder'n I thought.*

He paused and looked back at the encampment, saw the faint trail that had been used by the lookout and followed it below, approaching the camp slowly and cautiously. He worked his way behind two lodges and approached the one on higher ground. The piebald was standing hipshot on the far side and did not move as Ezra quietly stepped behind the wickiup. He pulled a small pouch from his belt, opened the drawstring, and moved close to the back of the brush hut. He poured the black power into the woven branches and in a small pile at the bottom edge. He emptied the pouch and stuffed it back in his belt. From his pocket, he withdrew the flint and steel, looked around, touched the pistol, and lifted it slightly to ensure it wasn't hooked on anything, then stepped near the powder. He held the big chunk of flint tightly and struck the steel across its face, drawing sparks downward onto the black powder. The powder hissed and flared, grey smoke pillared up and the hot flash of fire lit the dry sticks that flared into flame. Ezra had moved with the first strike and stood beside the doorway. He heard a mumbling from within and readied himself. The blanket covering was flipped aside and the bent-over figure of Singing Dog started to rise but the heavy barrels of the pistol crashed down on the back of his neck and head and he dropped to his face, unmoving.

Ezra grabbed Dog's long hair and dragged him back into the wickiup. He saw a woman starting to rise from her blankets and snarled at her, "Don't move!" as he pointed the pistol at her. Her eyes flared but she did not move, looking from Ezra to the back of the wickiup. Smoke was starting to fill the lodge but Ezra could see enough from the smoldering fire in the middle of the wickiup, the moonlight coming through the doorway, and the limited light from the slow-growing fire at the back of the lodge. He quickly looked around, spotted his rifle and war club laying on his tunic, and dropped to one knee beside them. He threatened the woman again, then quickly slipped his tunic over his head, hung his powder horn and possibles bag over his head and shoulders, and grabbed his rifle and war club. He looked for the pistol, then to the woman. He shook the pistol and asked, "Where?"

She pointed to the far side of the blankets and reached over to pick it up by the barrel. Smoke was starting to fill the structure as Ezra went to the woman, snatched up some cord beside the blankets, and turned her around. He tied her hands behind her back, then tied her feet together. He stuffed a piece of blanket in her mouth and bound it with the cord. He wrapped the blanket around her, put her under one arm, the rifle slung over his back, the two pistols in his belt, and the war club in the other hand and looked out the doorway, then stepped through. He went behind the lodge, set the woman down away from the smoldering hut and went to the far side where the now skittish piebald was pulling at his tether, trying to escape the smoke. He slipped the tether and swung aboard the animal and started through the camp. He was past most of the lodges when the wickiup flared up in tall flames, illuminating the area around. He thought about the leader, wondering if he was dead or would escape, *Prob'ly shoulda made sure he was dead!* He thought as he nudged the piebald to a faster pace toward the far lodge with the women.

Gabe moved silently, the horses following easily. He sat aboard Ebony, the bay beside him and the grey and mule following close behind. The mule's lead line was secured to the pack of the grey and the grey's lead line secured to the pommel of Ebony. The reins of the bay were looped loosely through the tie-down straps beside the cantle of Gabe's saddle and each were at a comfortable distance. Gabe watched the encampment as he moved past the upper end, the nearest wickiup about thirty yards away, and kept moving past the selected wickiup and to the edge of the river. He slipped down, loosely tethering Ebony to a spreading mesquite at water's edge, motioned Wolf to stay with the horses, and started back to the lodge, Mongol bow with nocked arrow in hand. His quiver hung at his side, his Bailes double-barreled pistol in his belt.

He dropped to one knee beside some sage to look over the still camp. His movements had not disturbed the sounds of the night and he listened to nearby bullfrogs, a circling nighthawk, and cicadas further back towards the arroyo. He rose in a crouch, started toward the nearby wickiup but was stayed when he caught movement near the river. He slowly dropped beside the sage, watching, as he saw a man coming from the willows, followed closely by a woman. When they came from the cover of the willows, they parted, looking at one another, and went to different wickiups. Gabe shook his head, knowing that was a rendezvous that would not be approved but glad that their attention was on other things. As they moved away and went into their individual lodges, he waited a moment, just to see if they had been caught, then chuckled to himself and started to the wickiup.

He stood near the opening, looking toward the other brush huts, then turned and slowly lifted the blanket, laying it back and catching on the brush. He slowly looked inside, concerned about a guard or other women that were watching, but there were two forms, both sitting up beside one another, staring back at Gabe. Their hands were tied behind their back and their feet were bound. He stepped inside, put a finger to his mouth, and spoke softly in Spanish, "I'm here to take you away!"

He slipped a knife from the scabbard that hung at his back, quickly cut their bonds, and smiled at their frightened expressions. He spoke softly, "When we go out, we must move quietly and go that way toward the river. I have horses there and you two will ride one together. Hopefully, my friend will bring more. Now, we must move quietly. Can you walk alright?"

They looked at one another, nodded, and rose tenuously to their feet, helping each other and holding to one another. Gabe turned and stepped to the doorway, looked out, stepped out and motioned the girls to move. He stood before the opening as they slipped away and started for the river.

Suddenly there was a cry from the far side of the camp and flames leaped from a wickiup near the ridge. More cries sounded and the wickiups regurgitated warriors and women, all looking toward the flaming lodge. Gabe started to turn away just as he heard a shout and saw a man pointing at him and start in his direction. Gabe lifted the bow and sent the arrow whispering toward its target. The shaft buried itself in the man's chest, driving him backwards and silencing him. He fell against his wickiup and slid to the ground, wide eyes sightless.

Gabe nocked another arrow, went to a crouch, and searched the encampment for any other alarm, then trotted into the darkness toward the river. The young women were standing beside the horses, holding to one another as they stared at Wolf. They looked back toward Gabe and he quickly spoke, "Get on the bay," motioning to Ezra's horse, "We'll cross the river!" He stepped into the stirrup, swung aboard the black, tossed the rein to the now mounted girls, and started to the river. It was a gravelly bottomed crossing that showed much use with a trail rising from the water to the trees beyond. Wolf led the way, splashing into the water and paddling against the current. With the water not quite belly deep on the horses, they made the crossing quickly and were soon on solid ground. Gabe paused to look back for Ezra and saw his friend aboard the piebald and entering the water. He turned and dug heels to the black, turned to the girls, "C'mon!"

They took to the trees, following a game trail that wound its way through the rolling knobs and ridges that appeared to be ancient, falling of the edge of the mesa, but it afforded a good trail to the top. Near the top, the rimrock blocked their way prompting them to move along the bottom of the rock until a cut made by spring run-off offered a way to the top. Within moments, they crested the big mesa and turned to look back on the encampment. They saw the burning wickiup was now nothing but smoldering ashes but there were some men leading several horses from the horse herd into the encampment. Several were shouting and screaming war cries and Gabe and Ezra knew this fight was not over. Gabe turned to the girls, "Do you have family?"

"The Apache killed our mother and father!" spat the girl aboard the saddle. She appeared to be a little older than the other girl who sat behind the cantle, holding tight to the tie-down straps.

"You're sisters?" asked Gabe.

"Yes! But they killed our family!"

"Do you have aunts, uncles, others?"

The older girl turned to look at her sister, they spoke quietly to one another, then turned back to Gabe, "Our mother's sister is in Santa Cruz."

"And where is Santa Cruz?" asked Gabe.

The girl pointed to the southwest, "There, where the rivers meet!"

"Well, after this is over, we'll take you there. But right now, I think we're gonna have company pretty soon." He paused, looking around, then back at the girls, "Do you know if there's a way off this mesa down that way?" pointing to the southwest end.

"I think so. If there is, we can find it."

"So, how 'bout you taking our pack animals and start that way. We'll stay back and see if we can discourage these Apache."

The older girl nodded, accepted the lead line of the grey and slapped legs to the bay to start across the long mesa. Gabe looked at Ezra, "Guess we better load up and find us a place to hunker down!"

26 / CONFLICT

"He is a Ga'an!" shouted *lichi chish kaaldi,* Red Woodpecker. He grabbed the woman of Singing Dog, "Tell the chief he was black! And he saved you!" The timid and grieving woman nodded, "But he let Singing Dog die in the fire!" she snarled, glaring at Woodpecker. He looked from the woman to the chief, White Wolf, and appealed to *yos tso',* White Shell, the shaman of the village. "If we go after him, many will die! He is big and powerful! Singing Dog had taken his great war club but he has taken it back! We cannot go against a Ga'an! It will cause many to die!" he pleaded.

White Shell looked from Woodpecker to the chief, scowling and shaking his head, "The black Ga'an is a protector of the people. He would only kill to protect the people!" The chief looked from his shaman to Woodpecker and motioned to a nearby warrior with a wave of his hand. They knew that meant for him to gather the warriors and go after the one who killed their war leader and stole his horse and plunder.

Woodpecker continued his argument, "He killed Singing Dog to protect the people. We had lost more than one hand of warriors to this white man that sends arrows farther than any other warrior. If Singing Dog had listened, they would not have died! The Ga'an has warned us!"

A young man ran up to the chief, shouting and pointing toward the lower encampment. White Wolf scowled, his nostrils flaring and the muscles in his cheeks flexing as he turned to face Woodpecker. "Enough!" he growled. "These men have killed another of our warriors and stolen the captive women!" He waved his arm to Woodpecker, "Go!"

The warriors had brought the horses into the encampment and were gathering their weapons and painting their faces. Several quickly slapped paint on their horses, some with handprints on the shoulders, others making lightning bolts down the legs, some making spots on the rumps of the animals.

White Wolf slipped the quiver over his head and shoulder, moved the strung bow beside the quiver then swung aboard his dapple-grey stallion, accepting his lance from his woman. The lance held several scalp locks and two feathers and served as much as a coup stick as a war lance. He lifted the lance high, shouting to the warriors and slapped legs to the grey and started for the river at a canter.

Their night vision had been hindered by the flames of the lodge and the shadows were all the darker for it but they knew the land and charged toward the river. They made the crossing, crowding one another, but the moonlight showed the turned soil from the horses of the attackers. The chief turned toward the warriors, lifted his lance, and screamed his war cry as he turned to kick his horse into a run, charging up the hilly slope.

The horses dug deep, humping their backs as they fought for footing, gasping for air and lunging up the rough hillside. There were fifteen warriors, all searching for their own path through the brush and sage, circumventing the scraggly piñons, slapping their legs to their mount's ribs, leaning well over the neck to give balance, and talking to their horses, continually encouraging them.

Suddenly, several screams and shouts, that were not war cries, alarmed the riders. They looked up the hillside and saw flames licking at the trees and brush and showering the air with embers. The roar of the fire swept over them and they began searching for an escape. The horses were immediately frightened and fought their riders, naturally yielding to the need of self-preservation, rearing up, fighting the reins and shouts of the riders, twisting around, seeking an escape. The confusion and pandemonium added to the fear of the fire and horses tumbled over backwards, feet kicking at the air, adding their own screams to those of the warriors. Unseated riders were running down the hill, one man overrun by a riderless horse, others fought to keep control of their animals but all yielding to the natural fear of fire.

Within moments, the mighty warriors of the Jicarilla Apache renegade band were running away, screaming in fear, splashing into the water, and fighting one another for their escape. When several mounted the far bank, they slipped from their horses, falling on their faces in the wet grass, sucking for air, and gasping for breath. They looked around at the others, turned their attention to the fire that had swept down the hillside, consuming everything in its path, and watched the rising cloud of smoke as it caught the first light of morning.

As the smoke began to clear White Wolf stood beside his shaman, White Shell, looking across the river at the black scarred hillside. He nodded, "Two horses, three warriors." He was looking at the charred remains of the horses and men as he spoke. He looked at his shaman, "Was this a Ga'an?"

The shaman looked at his chief, shaking his head, "When the people rise against the spirits, death always follows."

* * * * *

Gabe turned back and nudged Ebony along the top edge of the mesa, overlooking the river and valley below. The moonlight showed shadows of terraces at the top of the rolling hilly shoulder they had just climbed. It was the rimrock at the edge of the lower of three terraces that detoured them to the run-off cut. Below the bottom terrace, the hills were thick with buffalo grass, sage and mostly thick scrub oak brush. Gabe stepped down and Ezra joined him at the edge, looking below, calculating what would be their best defense. They looked at the village, saw the warriors working themselves into a frenzy, gathering their horses near and shouting and screaming war cries.

"They'll be coming right soon!" declared Ezra.

"Ummhmmm," responded Gabe, looking below. He stood, "Maybe we should light the way for 'em."

Ezra stood, frowning, "Light the way?"

Gabe turned back toward the flat top of the mesa, "Feel that?" he said as he wet a finger and lifted it head high. The cool morning breeze whispered in from the far mountains, moving across the mesa toward the river valley below. "With that at our backs . . ." and turned to look below. "Let's go!" he declared and swung aboard Ebony, swinging him around to the cut that brought them to the top. Within moments Gabe was leaning far back against the cantle of his saddle, feet in the stirrups and extended along the shoulders and neck of his horse as the animals plunged down the steep cut to be stopped at the edge of the lower terrace. Ezra lay back on the rump of the piebald, tucked his toes behind the front legs, and stretched out, doing his best to keep from sliding over the withers. Gabe turned Ebony to follow the rimrock across the face of the broad hilly shoulder and stopped, stepped down and looked at the brush. Ezra joined him, "Now what?"

"Gather the driest brush and weeds, pile 'em high at the edge of the buck brush. Make several piles, quick!"

Both men scampered about the edge of the brush, occasionally glancing to the encampment to see what the warriors were doing, but hurriedly gathering armloads of dry brush. Within moments, they had made six thick piles, chest high, and Gabe went to the pile furthest from the cut. He gathered a handful of dry buffalo grass, wrapping it around the end of a stick, and with a glance to Ezra, "Get your flint and steel!"

Gabe knelt near the bottom of the brush pile, held the crude torch near and waited while Ezra began striking the flint with the steel. Sparks showered the brush, started to smolder and Gabe bent close to blow on the sparks. Ezra had looked below, "Here they come!"

Gabe sheltered the tiny flame, blew a little more,

and as it flared, he lit the torch, "Go!" he ordered Ezra, "Here, take Ebony!" and handed him the reins. He knew the natural tendency of a fire is to move uphill, but he was counting on the breeze coming over the top of the mesa to drive it down toward the river. Ezra swung aboard the piebald, slapped legs to the horse's ribs and the big stallion lunged forward, pulling Ebony behind. Gabe sheltered the torch with his hand and hurried to the next pile, ignited the brush, and moved to the next. Within moments, all six piles were flaring and the breeze began to push the fire into the brush.

A wave of fire grew and moved in a ragged line toward the bottom of the hill, pushed by the breeze that seemed to be increasing with the flames. Gabe swung aboard Ebony, turned back to look at the warriors who were in a frenzy, some wanting to find a way through the flames, most just hanging on to their horses as the frightened animals, eyes wide and nostrils flaring, reared up and turned away from the charging maelstrom of flames, seeking escape in the river.

Gabe dug heels into Ebony's ribs and followed Ezra up the steep draw of the cut to reach the crest of the mesa. When they topped out, they turned to look behind to see if any of the Apache had made it to the cut but there were none. They rode together along the edge of the mesa to look at the burning hillside but the fast-moving flames had consumed most of the dry brush and smoke rose high, catching the beginning light of the new day. The river was crowded with riders and horses, several already riding into the encampment.

"Guess they didn't 'preciate you 'lightin' the way' for 'em!" drawled Ezra as they turned away to follow the two girls.

27 / MESA

Gabe and Ezra kicked the horses into a canter, following the easy-to-read sign of the two girls and the packhorses. They stayed close to the south edge of the mesa, often looking into the wide canyon of the Rio Bravo, or Rio Grande as many were calling it, and watching the rimrock edge for a passageway down. They passed several places where it appeared that in some ancient time the rimrock had sluffed off and tumbled below, leaving a sort of land bridge that offered trails to the bottom, but the tracks of their horses and the girls continued to the west toward the far end of the mesa.

They dropped the horses into a walk, giving them a breather, and Gabe turned in his saddle to look behind them for any pursuit but there was nothing but thin dust behind them. As he turned back, he glanced to Ezra, "Guess we discouraged 'em! Nobody's behind us!"

"That's good. Should be catchin' up to the girls soon, don't ya reckon?"

"Yeah, judgin' from the tracks," began Gabe, motioning to the fresh tracks they followed, "I reckon they're maybe a mile or two ahead of us. Prob'ly waitin' up there somewhere." He saw Wolf sitting beside the trail, waiting for them, tongue lolling and eyes bright as if to say, "What took you so long?" Gabe chuckled at the thought knowing the big wolf communicated with his expressions better than most people with words. As they came near, Wolf started off on the trail ahead of them but kept to a slow pace so as to not outdistance the men.

They were within sight of the west point of the mesa when they spotted the girls and horses at a cluster of juniper near the beginning of a dry bed run-off. Behind the trees, the dry creek bed had channeled its way through some basalt and sandstone and the resulting watershed had given moisture that resulted in considerable growth of piñon, cedar, and juniper as well as some stunted mesquite. There was ample shade and Gabe and Ezra quickly dismounted and went to the shady site where the girls were seated on the slight slope beneath the juniper.

"Are the Apache coming?" asked the older girl, fear showing in her eyes.

Gabe chuckled, "No, I think we discouraged them from following. At least for now." He looked from one to the other, and added, "I'm Gabe," motioning to himself, then with a wave toward his friend, "And this is Ezra."

The girl smiled, "I am Gabriella de Onate and this is my sister, Isabella."

"Ladies," replied both Gabe and Ezra, nodding to the girls.

"We are grateful to you señors, for rescuing us from the Apache. We were very afraid."

Gabe nodded as he and Ezra seated themselves opposite the girls, but still in the shade, "You said the Apache killed your mother and father, were there others at your home?"

"No, señor. But they attacked our neighbors and killed them also."

"And you said your mother has a sister at Santa Cruz?"

"Si, señor. It has been a long time since we saw our aunt and she has married. We think her married name is Elena Esquibel."

"But you're not sure?" asked Ezra, frowning.

"We think so but we could be wrong."

"Do you know where she lives?" asked Gabe.

"No, señor. But the padre at the church will know."

"The church? There's a church there?"

"Si, señor. The church has been there a long time. Our father and mother were married in that church."

Gabe looked at Ezra, disbelieving, but shrugged

and turned back to the girls. "How 'bout we have a little something to eat and give the horses a bit of a rest before we start down into the valley?"

"Would you like us to cook you something?" asked Isabella, smiling, and scooting forward to show her eagerness.

Gabe looked at Ezra, back at the girls, "Well, let's see what we have and then decide, all right?"

It took little encouragement for Ezra to get a pot of water boiling for some coffee and the girls were soon eagerly preparing some corn cakes with strips of smoked meat boiling in the pot with the onions, potatoes, and more that the girls had gathered nearby. Gabe sat close to the fire, watching the girls busy at their task, Ezra watching the coffeepot dance and the quiet they shared in the shade. As he observed the girls, he guessed them to be about twelve and thirteen summers old, maybe a little older. He lifted his eyes to Gabriella and asked, "So, how old are you girls?"

Gabriella smiled, "I am soon to be fourteen and Isabella is twelve. In our community, we both would be considered old enough to be betrothed." She dropped her eyes and Gabe saw a lone tear make its path through the dust on her cheeks.

Isabella glanced at her and turned her attention back to the pot she stirred. Tears filled her eyes as she tried hard to not let them fall. She stifled a sob and looked up at Gabe and over to Ezra and asked, "Why?"

"Why? Why did I ask how old you were?"

"No, why did this happen. My parents never hurt anyone and were always helpful to all our neighbors. Why did God let this happen to them?"

Gabe dropped his gaze, shuffling his feet in the dirt, struggling to find an answer, then glanced at Ezra, "I think I'll let Ezra try to answer that for you. He knows more about those things than I do."

Ezra frowned, shook his head slightly and lowered his head and closed his eyes, his lips moving in an urgent prayer. He looked up at the girls, took a deep breath that lifted his shoulders, then began, "We can never know the why of many things until the day we stand before the Lord and ask Him but I will try to answer the best I know how." He paused, gathering his thoughts, and continued, "Before you were taken by the Apache, they had taken me captive. I was bound and tied to my horse and led by one of the warriors around the butte near your rancho. That was when they attacked your place but that was also when Gabe there, was able to rescue me from the Apache. If he had not been able to do that, we would not have been able to rescue you." He looked from one to the other, "If your father was like I think he was, he would have gladly given his life to make sure you girls were spared and delivered from the Apache. But I think it's more than that. You see, God has a plan, a purpose, for each of us, and He gives us the time and opportunity to fulfill that plan."

The girls frowned, looking to one another and back to Ezra as Gabriella asked, "But how do we know that plan?"

Ezra let a slow smile cross his face, "Well, first, we have to know Him."

Isabella chimed in, "But we know Him. Doesn't everyone?"

"It's not to just know who He is, it's to know him as your personal savior. You see, you know about Jesus on the cross, don't you?"

Both girls nodded and scooted a little closer, listening attentively, as Gabe assumed their task of tending to the meal.

Ezra went to his saddlebags and brought out the Bible and returned to the girls' side as he opened it to the book of I John, chapter five, "You see, here in verse thirteen it says, *These things have I written unto you that believe on the name of the Son of God,"* He looked at the girls and asked, "You believe in Jesus, don't you?"

The girls nodded enthusiastically and Ezra continued, "So, this was written to you but it goes on to tell us why, *"That ye may know that ye have eternal life . . .* the eternal life he mentions is for us to know Heaven as our home and to live for all eternity with Him. We can't live eternally here," motioning around to the surrounding terrain, "and He wants us to have that eternal life. He also says in John chapter five and verse twenty-four, *He that heareth my word, and believeth on him that sent me, hath everlasting life and shall not come into condemnation; but is passed from death unto life."* He paused, looking to the girls and saw questions in their eyes. He grinned slightly and continued, "That everlasting life is the same as eternal life, to live forever with Him. And if we have it, we'll not see condemnation or hell and judgment but we're passed right over that unto life forever. He tells us in the first part, that we must *heareth my word, and believeth on him.* Let me explain," he stood and walked to the piebald and led him back near the girls. He looked at the horse, walked around him, stroked his neck and head, and turned to the girls.

"Do you believe this is a horse?"

The girls giggled and Gabriella answered, "Of course!"

Ezra grinned, "I do to! This is a horse. I believe this is a horse. I believe this horse can hold me and carry me wherever I want to go but is this horse holding me now?"

Isabella frowned, "No, but I don't understand."

Ezra grabbed a handful of mane and swung aboard the horse. Once seated astride, he leaned back, patted the animal on the rump, then nudged him forward and reined him around in a circle. "Now, is this horse holding me up and taking me where he wants?"

"Yes," said a frowning Gabriella.

"That is the difference," began Ezra as he slid to the ground. "Anyone can believe he is a horse but it is only when you *trust* your belief and put your confidence and belief to work and get on him, will you have any benefit." He paused, "That's what the scripture means when it says, *He that heareth my word, and believeth on him.* It's not just believing that there was a Jesus, it's putting your belief to work and putting all your trust in Him to take you to Heaven when you die and to guide you while you live."

He sat down across from them, giving them a moment to consider what he said, then added, "It is a special step we take to accept Jesus as our Savior. That how we put our trust in Him. He offers us the gift of eternal life, a gift we do not deserve, so He paid for it on the cross when He died for our sins. Now He offers you that gift and all you have to do is put your trust in Him by calling on Him in prayer. Do you understand that?"

The girls looked at one another, then to Ezra and nodded. Isabella asked, "Will you help us?"

"Of course. Here's what I will do. I will pray and, as I pray, I will give you the opportunity to pray and if you believe it with all your heart and mean it, then you can pray with me." The girls enthusiastically nodded and as Ezra bowed his head and closed his eyes, they did the same.

He began, "Our Father in Heaven, we come to you now to ask you for the free gift of eternal life purchased for us on the cross of Calvary by your son, Jesus." He spoke to the girls, "Now if you mean it, say it after me . . .Forgive me of my sins and come into my heart and be my savior. I want to trust you today to take me to heaven when I die and to guide me while I live for you. In Jesus name, Amen."

The girls had joined with Ezra and prayed the prayer. After the Amen, they looked up, smiling and with tears streaming down their faces, they hugged one another and together hugged Ezra, almost knocking him over as they laughed and rejoiced together. As he sat up, he grew somber and added, "Now, just so you know, when hard times come our way and we don't understand the why of it, that's when we need to *trust* the way of it. Remember, God always has His purpose and plan in everything and that's when we learn to *trust*."

Gabe chuckled and laughed with them, "Well with that being done, how 'bout we eat?"

Again with the laughter but they all joined hands together around the small fire and thanked the Lord for their safety, the food, their deliverance, and the gift of eternal life. When they finished, the girls were chattering as they helped with the clean-up and Ezra went to the horses to saddle and pack.

Gabe had taken the scope to the rimrock edge and was having a look-see to the valley below and to their back trail. And it was a somber Gabe that returned to the cookfire. He sat down in the shade, leaned back on one elbow, and waited for Ezra to come near. "Them soldier boys from the garrison at Santa Fe are headin' toward the camp of the Apache." He paused, thinking, "You don't suppose they're gonna hit 'em?"

Ezra scowled at his friend, "After what we saw of that Lieutenant, it's hard tellin' what they'll be doin'," started Ezra, as he turned to look at Gabe, "But one thing I do know, that Apache leader and his sidekick were talkin' a couple times and I heard them use the word Lieutenant when they were lookin' my direction. His right-hand man was also talkin' 'bout the comancheros. I got the feelin' they were plannin' on tradin' me to the Lieutenant for some soldier guns and he'd trade me to the comancheros."

"So, it's like we thought. The Lieutenant is in the business of buyin' and sellin' captives."

"I reckon."

"Then I reckon we need to get these girls down to the church or somewhere so we can put this country behind us!" declared Gabe, rising, and going to the horses to finish gearing up.

28 / SANTA CRUZ

The soldados were an impressive sight as they rode into the rancheria of the Apache. The Lieutenant sat erect and tall in the saddle, his brass buttons shining and braided epaulets dancing. He naturally assumed his arrogant superior attitude as he looked down on the many grieving women with children at their sides. Warriors stood beside their wickiups, glaring at the intruders, but they were a familiar sight having visited their encampment many times before. A recognizable face looked at the cavalcade, prompting the Lieutenant to stop and order, "Tell Singing Dog and White Wolf that Lieutenant Delgado demands their presence!"

Woodpecker stepped closer, looking up at the leader of the soldados, glanced back at the men and returned his stare to the leader. "White Wolf knows you are here. If you want to see him, go to his lodge!"

"Where is Singing Dog?" snarled the Lieutenant.

"He is dead!" snapped Woodpecker.

The Lieutenant frowned, looked around at the curious members of the tribe, noted several grieving women, "Why are they wailing?" he demanded, pointing his quirt toward two women that held their children close as they wept.

"They weep for their men who died following your friend," answered Woodpecker, purposefully failing to use the name of the dead war leader. Many natives refused to use the name of anyone that has died believing it would call the evil side of their spirit back into their presence.

The officer glared at Woodpecker and again demanded, "Tell White Wolf I am here!"

Woodpecker looked at the man, glanced to the far edge of the encampment, nodding as he said, "His lodge is the one with crossed lances," and turned away and walked through the wickiups to distance himself from the soldados.

The Lieutenant snarled, slapped the quirt to the rump of his horse and started toward the chief's wickiup. As he neared, the chief stepped out and stood, arms crossed as he looked at the leader of the soldados. White Shell stepped beside him, assuming a similar stance. The officer leaned forward, crossing his forearms on the pommel of his saddle, and hissed, "Singing Dog promised to have a captive or captives for me!"

"The one you speak of is no longer with us! We are not bound by his promises. We have nothing for you!" growled White Wolf.

The Lieutenant straightened up, slapped his leg with the quirt, "The governor of Santa Fe has said I am to capture or kill those raiders who attacked the hacienda at the point of rocks by the river Chama! That was Singing Dog and his warriors!"

"Tell your governor that the leader of that raid and many of his warriors are dead! We have lost many of our warriors! You hear the women wailing their sorrow! Tell that to your governor!" He then motioned toward the wickiups and the trail that followed the Rio Bravo downstream. Beside and between the many lodges stood warriors, arrows nocked in their bows or lances lifted to throw. At a glance, the Lieutenant knew if the warriors were given the command, most if not all of his men, with their rifles in the scabbards and their pistols in their holsters, would be killed. In his eagerness to gain the captive black man, he had led his men into a trap.

White Wolf barked, "Leave our village or you will die!"

The Lieutenant looked back at the chief, shook his head and struggled to keep his tongue as he reined his mount around and gave the hand signal for the men to follow and did his best to sit tall and dignified as he led the soldados from the village. Sergeant de Abrego rode up beside Delgado, "What do we do now, Lieutenant?"

"The Alcalde said we were to go to Santa Cruz to find the raiders. We will go there and return to Santa Fe to tell the governor the raiders have been killed!"

"But the soldados . . ." began the Sergeant.

"They will not mind a night in Santa Cruz," suggested the officer, nodding to the Sergeant as they both remembered other excursions into the old town and the cantinas.

* * * * *

An ancient trail showed itself just the other side of the deep arroyo that cut through the rimrock and plunged down the steep slope. The trail of ancients, an easy trail that twisted through the scraggly piñon and cedar, rode the crest of a long shoulder that turned into a high ridge and dropped them into the flats beside the dry creek bed. With the sun high overhead, they covered the two miles off the mesa and onto the flats in a short while. Another mile brought them near the banks of the Rio Chama and they stepped down to let the horses have a good drink. The greenery and tall cottonwoods offered a respite from the hot sun and they were in no hurry to leave.

When Gabe swung aboard, the others were slow

to mount, the girls now on the piebald and Ezra back in the saddle aboard his bay. They pushed on, staying near the grassy shores of the river but away from the thicker mesquite, alders, and cottonwoods. When the girls spotted a patch of raspberries, they were quick to jump down and start gathering the handfuls in their skirts. Ezra handed them a partially empty parfleche and they soon had a good supply. They offered a handful to each of the men, secured the parfleche on the mule, and swung back aboard the piebald.

Another couple miles brought them within sight of the banks of the Rio Bravo, which prompted Gabe to take to a nearby rise and look upstream for the soldados. He returned shortly, shaking his head and spoke softly to Ezra, "Dunno. They could be coming this way but just be too far back to see or maybe they just went back to Santa Fe."

"No, they're comin'. I can feel it!" declared Ezra, giving Gabe the familiar look that told of his premonitions.

Wolf waited at the bank of the river, seated beside what was an obviously well-used crossing back from the confluence with the Rio Chama. They were about a mile upstream on the Rio Bravo above the confluence and the gravelly slopes on both sides of the river told of many crossings by wagons, probably the trade wagons to the village from the many haciendas and ranchos in the valley. Gabe knew this area had seen settlement by the Spaniards for over two hundred years and by the Tewa long before that. From his promontory when he looked for the soldados, he also spotted a pueblo, similar to the one where they left Slow Turtle, on the west side of the Rio Bravo.

As they neared the crossing, Gabe frowned, looking downstream toward the Rio Chama, "Say, that looks like the village where we left Slow Turtle and Red Nose. I think the pueblo was just downstream from this confluence."

Ezra looked where Gabe was looking, stood in his stirrups, "I think you're right. Appears to be 'bout the right location. Wonder if they're still there?"

"Dunno but, for right now, we've got other things to tend to!" and nudged Ebony into the water, pulling the lead line of the grey taut, as he watched Wolf splash into the murky water and start paddling across. The current was slow but strong, the water stirrup deep, but the horses seemed to enjoy the cool water and had little difficulty crossing. When they climbed out on the south side, all the riders stepped down and let the horses shake but kept them from rolling. Although the mule gave his best effort to have a good roll, Ezra discouraged the stubborn animal with a tight hold on his lead.

They passed several small ranchos with adobe houses and makeshift barns, most had goats, a milk cow, and horses and some a few more cows. All had well-tended gardens, a few had shade trees of cottonwood or mesquite, and the structures were usually close together, probably for defensive purposes. Most fields had men busy tending the crops, clotheslines near the houses had off-white clothing waving in the breeze, and children were usually working with the parents in the field or gardens.

The village of Santa Cruz de la Cañada lay a little more than five miles south of the confluence of the Rio Grande and the Rio Chama. Most of the *villa* was near the river by the same name. As they neared the village, Gabe and Ezra noted the many fruit orchards and the irrigation systems set up by the people. Ezra said, "We need to get us some fruit to take home!"

Gabe chuckled, "If any of it is ripe, we might!"

"Hey, right now, even a green apple would taste good," declared a grinning Ezra.

"The church is there, not far from the river," declared Gabriella, pointing to the south between two adobe structures that appeared to be businesses. Gabe noticed one had a sign *Herrero* and in smaller letters, *Establos de librea* and Gabe recognized it as a Blacksmith and Livery. They rode past the two buildings and saw an impressive church structure with two citadels with steeples and crosses. Surrounded by a low adobe wall, the church was well-tended and kept with tall juniper planted close by and more in the church yard.

They rode into the courtyard, tethered the horses at a hitch rail near the trees and stepped away from the animals as they attempted to slap the dust from their clothes. They walked toward the hand-carved double doors and Ezra stepped forward to pull one open. They stood in the shadow of the citadels for a moment, then stepped through the doorway into the dim interior. Sunlight filtered through the two windows on either side as well as the high window above the doorway. The window behind them illumined the heavy, hand-hewed beams that crossed high above. The white-washed walls were bare of any decoration and their eyes were drawn forward to the recessed altar. High above the pulpit arched a carved wooden canopy that sheltered the filigree and artwork that sided the small crucifix in the center of the back wall.

They stood hushed and still as a figure in dark brown monk's robes rose from the altar and turned to face them. His voice was bigger than his stature as he smiled and greeted them in Spanish, "Greetings my friends. Welcome to the church of Santa Cruz de la Cañada. I am Padre Mateo, how may I help you?" he spoke as he walked toward them, arms outstretched and open.

The men had removed their hats and their sweaty heads and hair glistened in the dim light. Gabe stepped forward, extending his hand, "Padre, I am Gabe, and my friend is Ezra. These girls," he turned slightly to look back at the girls, "are looking for the sister of their mother. Sadly, their parents were killed by the Apache and they were taken captive but only for a short while. Their only relation nearby is Elena Esquibel and we were hoping you could tell us where we might find her."

The padre listened attentively, frowning when he heard of the tragedy and wringing his hands as Gabe continued. When he heard the name Elena Esquibel, he nodded and smiled. "I am so sorry for your loss, girls, but yes, I do know Elena. She and her husband, Carlos, have a cantina not far from here. It is a fine cantina and they have excellent food. I'm sure they will be happy to see you."

"Also, Padre. . ." began Gabe, nodding to Ezra to take the girls outside. Once they were out of hearing, Gabe continued, "There is a Lieutenant of the garrison at Santa Fe. We had a run-in with him in Santa Fe and it seems he has followed us. My friend was taken captive by the Apache, like the girls, and he overheard them speaking of the Lieutenant and his trading for captives. I get the impression he wanted to enslave my friend and sell him to the comancheros or something."

"Yes, yes. We know of this man. He and his Sergeant are known to trade in captives and slaves and have done this many times. He is not a good man."

"You're right about that. But, the problem is, they

might be following us. We want to get the girls to their family and will be leaving right away but there's no telling what that soldier boy might try to do. I just thought it would be good for someone to know what was happening. My friend, Ezra, is not now nor has he ever been a slave. He is the freeborn son of the pastor of a large church in Philadelphia."

The padre listened and nodded as Gabe spoke, smiling when he heard of Ezra's being the son of a pastor. When Gabe finished, he asked, "And what has brought you to our territory?"

"We have families and a home up north, in the Rockies, and we came to Santa Fe to resupply. But we've run into the Apache a few times and now the Lieutenant and his soldados are making things a mite uncomfortable for us. We are on our way home to our families now."

"And you bought the girls from the Apache?" asked the padre.

"Oh no! We rescued them, had to sneak 'em outta the Apache village east of here. They followed us a spell but we discouraged 'em a mite."

Gabe looked around, "Mighty nice church you have here Padre."

"Thank you my son. This church has been here since 1733," he beamed.

"Almost as long as our church in Philadelphia!" replied Gabe. "But we need to be going and see if we can get the girls to their family. Thank you Padre, you've been very helpful."

"You are welcome, my son. And may God bless you on your journey home."

Gabe nodded and turned away to exit the church. Ezra and the girls waited just outside the door and as Gabe stepped to the walkway, they fell in beside him. Gabe glanced at the girls, "Are you excited to see your Aunt Elena?"

"Sort of, but she might not remember us. We don't remember much about her; it's been a long time since we were here," explained Gabriella.

29 / CONFRONTATION

They mounted up and reined the horses around to go back into the village to find the Cantina Esquibel and hopefully have a good welcome from the family. The small village made it easy to find the cantina and they tethered the horses at the hitch rail and stepped to the door just as a man stumbled out and caught himself on the hitchrail. He looked around, grinned, turned away and staggered down the walkway. Gabe and Ezra looked at one another, shaking their heads slightly in understanding and Gabe stepped through the door.

A man's voice hollered, "I told you . . ." then stopped as he looked up to see Gabe standing in the doorway. The filtered shafts of light from the two windows lanced toward the floor, revealing several tables with chairs, only one with a man seated. A lanky man near the doorway to the kitchen, a spotted apron across his middle and a wet rag in his hand, glared at Gabe, "What do you want?" he growled.

When Gabe paused in the doorway, the girls and Ezra stayed back and waited. Gabe now spoke, "I'm looking for Elena Esquibel."

"She's my woman. What do you want?"

"I would like to speak with her. I have something from her sister."

"That peasant! She has nothing we want!" snarled the man, stepping forward a little.

Gabe said, "May I speak with her?"

"No man speaks with my woman less I say so!" snarled the man. As he spoke, the doorway behind him was filled with a stocky figure that pushed hair from her face and tucked it behind her ear. Her black hair held a thin streak of grey, her eyes were lifeless, and her full cheeks hung over her jaws. Her lip curled and her nose snarled a little as she asked, "Who wants to talk to me?"

Gabe stepped forward, "Are you Elena Esquibel?"

"Yes."

"You are the sister of Margarite de Onate and the aunt of Gabriella and Isabella?"

"That's right, why?"

"Ma'am, I regret to tell you that your sister and her husband were killed in a raid by Apache."

The woman staggered a step, caught herself in the doorway as she put her hand to her mouth. She looked wide-eyed at Gabe as her husband came to her side to take hold of her arm to steady her. She looked at Gabe, "Her girls?"

Gabe stepped aside to show Gabriella and Isabella standing behind him. They timidly stepped into the cantina, glancing around, and looked at the portly woman that stared at them. Gabriella asked softly, "Aunt Elena?"

The woman caught her breath, grabbed at a hanky in her apron and put it to her mouth as she slowly stepped toward the girls. She held out her arms and the girls walked to her. She engulfed them in her bulk, holding them tight and sobbing. The girls struggled for air and leaned back away from the woman, Gabriella glancing at Gabe and Ezra.

The men sat at one of the tables, watching and listening as the woman and girls talked about what happened and about their parents. The woman, who just moments ago seemed to be an impatient and intolerant biddy, now took on the image of a doting grandmother. She looked up at Gabe, "We never had children of our own and I always envied my sister. This is a blessing from the Almighty, it is indeed."

"We have not known them long but they are very special girls and will need a lot of love to guide them in this life. Are you prepared for that?" asked Gabe, his concern for the girls evident.

"I have asked God many times for children and He

has brought my nieces to me. Yes, I am prepared to take care of them. Our home is big and they will have their own room and we will go out tomorrow and buy them some clothes and everything they need." She glanced at the girls, "I am so excited to have them in our home and, if they want, they can help us in the cantina but only if they want." She smiled broadly, patting the hand of Gabriella who smiled at her aunt. The girls seemed to relax while she talked and nudged one another when she spoke of clothes and more.

"What about your husband, he doesn't seem too happy about them," asked Ezra, glancing at the door of the kitchen where he had disappeared.

"Oh, he will learn. We," nodding and smiling at the girls, "will teach him!" she declared. She smiled at Gabe, "Now, would you like something to eat?"

Gabe glanced at Ezra, "You want to get something to eat before we skedaddle?"

Ezra just grunted, shaking his head in disbelief that Gabe would even ask such a foolish question, nodded his head as he grinned at the woman. She nodded back and started to the kitchen, leaving the girls at the table after reassuring them she would get them some food as well.

She had no more risen than Carlos, her husband, stepped into the room, glaring at her and the others. Elena did not hesitate and walked to him, snatched the wet rag from his hand and twirled it around and snapped it at his leg. The resounding slap was almost like a gunshot and the man jumped and yelled but, before his feet touched the floor, she snapped him again and again, making him dance his way back into the kitchen. Gabe glanced at Ezra and both men burst out in laughter and noticed the girls laughing as well. The girls stood and returned to the table with Gabe and Ezra, laughing as they listened to the one-sided discussion from the kitchen. The yelping and snapping continued along with a rather robust argument with almost all the talking coming from the woman.

Within moments, a recalcitrant Carlos, head hanging and arms full, came into the cantina and set full platters before the girls and Gabe and Ezra. He averted his eyes, mumbled something unintelligible and quickly returned to the kitchen. A smiling Elena stepped through the doorway and came to their table, looked at the men, "My husband, Carlos, was just telling me how happy he is that the girls will be coming to live with us. He is just as excited as I am and we will be going to church to pray and thank the Lord for his goodness. And we are very grateful to you two for being so kind as to bring our darling girls to our home."

It was all Gabe and Ezra could do to keep a straight face but they looked at one another then to Elena, "I am certain you will make a very fine family. Don't you think so, Girls?" asked Gabe.

"Oh, yes. It will be wonderful to live with Aunt Elena," said a smiling Gabriella.

The woman stepped close and stood between the girls, resting a hand on their shoulders, and agreed, "It will be wonderful, I promise," she reassured. She turned away to return to the kitchen but the door opened, and she turned to greet the newcomers. Gabe glanced up from his plate to see the Lieutenant and First Sergeant step into the cantina. He paused as he brought the tortilla to his mouth, nudging a very hungry and busy Ezra with his elbow. When Ezra looked at Gabe, then to the door, he paused in his eating and glared at the uniformed men as they stepped in and started toward a table.

When their eyes had adjusted to the dim light, both the Lieutenant and the Sergeant paused as they recognized Gabe and Ezra. A slow grin split Delgado's face as he stepped closer to Gabe and Ezra's table. He glanced at the girls then to the men, "Well, well. We meet again. But this time there is no Pedro Vial to intercede for you." He looked at his Sergeant, "What do you think Sergeant, should we take them now, or wait until we eat?"

"Whatever you say, Lieutenant, but I have been looking forward to a good meal," replied Sergeant de Abrego.

"Very well, Sergeant. I am a little hungry, myself." He snarled as he looked from Gabe to the girls, "What have we here? Aren't these a little young for you?"

Ezra started to rise but Gabe gave him a quick glance to keep his seat, then turned to look at the officer, "I don't see how anything we do is any of your business, sonny," as he took another bite.

The Lieutenant stepped forward, but restrained himself, laughed, "We will tend to you later!" he growled, then moved away to go to a table on the far side of the room.

Elena had watched the confrontation, keeping her distance, then went to the men as they seated themselves. She told them of the items available, accepted their order, and turned back to the kitchen with a surreptitious glance toward Gabe. But Gabe remained seated and spoke quietly to Gabriella and sent her to the kitchen to explain to her aunt.

Gabe continued to eat as if nothing was amiss and he and Ezra spoke softly. "I don't want to involve the girls or their aunt in this but we can't just sit here and wait for them to do whatever they're planning."

"You know what they're planning. They want to claim I'm a runaway slave and they'll sell me to the highest bidder and I ain't gonna let that happen!" growled Ezra who continued to work at the remains on his plate.

The door opened again and the padre stepped into the room, looked for Gabe and Ezra and came immediately to their table. He nodded to the girls, accepted the chair offered by Ezra and started to speak but noted Gabe had his finger before his lips as he slowly nodded toward the Lieutenant and his Sergeant. The padre leaned forward, "I was afraid of that. When I learned the soldados had come into the *villa,* I walked the streets and saw where they went. All the others are in the other cantinas, they are more of a tavern than cantina, the men go there to have their tequila and to meet the señoritas. They are not like here where it is for the food." He glanced around, looked at Gabe, "Is there anything I can do?"

Gabe looked at Ezra and back to the padre, "I'm not sure what we'll do but you might not want to be here. However, after we leave, you might hunt up the next man in charge and tell him his Lieutenant and First Sergeant are indisposed and they will have to return to Santa Fe without them."

The wide-eyed padre looked at Gabe and to Ezra, then started, "You're not . . ."

Gabe grinned, "We'll be a gentle as possible. But we will not be taken by these slave traders, nor will anyone else."

The padre nodded and slowly rose, looking around and, intentionally avoiding the soldados, walked out of the cantina. Gabriella returned to the table and sat down, glanced at the officer and sergeant then resumed eating. With her back to the soldiers, she whispered, "Aunt Elena was very angry when I told her about the soldiers buying and selling captives and what they would have done with us. She said she will distract them while you leave or whatever you want to do."

"Good, now let's just wait and see," replied Gabe as he wiped his plate clean with the last tortilla.

30 / ESCAPE

Dusk had snuffed the day's lantern that left golden shafts lingering above the western hills. The three-quarter moon rose proudly in the eastern sky, taking its place in the darkening canopy as a few timid stars lit their lanterns. A lone candle sat atop the clay jug in the midst of the table where the blue and red uniformed soldiers waited for their food. The Lieutenant sat stiffly, always cognizant of his dignity and superiority, at least so he thought. The First Sergeant sat with elbows on the table as he glared at the men on the far side of the cantina's room. Two other tables that held hungry men had emptied and the only ones remaining were the adversaries who snatched glances at one another.

The door to the kitchen was filled with the big woman, both hands full of platters and followed by her husband with a big pot of hot coffee. She winked at Gabe as she passed his table and Gabe nodded to Ezra. As the woman neared the table, she laughed, smiling at the men, and started to set the first platter down in front of the Lieutenant while at the same time her husband stepped beside the Sergeant to pour a cup of coffee. With a slight nod to her husband, she stumbled and threw both platters of food at the Lieutenant, hitting him full in the face with the first one and filling his lap with the second. The food was piping hot and the officer jumped back, screaming as he grabbed at his face.

Carlos had followed his wife's lead and splashed the cup of coffee on the Sergeant's face and emptied the pot against his chest and lap. He too jumped to his feet, grabbing at his face and slapping at his pants and chest. Both men were shouting and cursing as they tried to dance away from the scalding food and coffee but Gabe and Ezra were ready and brought the barrels of their pistols crashing down on the back of the men's heads. Both crumpled in a heap on the floor.

The girls had been given the job of leaving the cantina and retrieving blankets from the packhorse. Gabriella grabbed the blankets, glanced down the roadway to see if any other soldiers were outside and, seeing none, darted back into the cantina, as Isabella barred the door. Gabe was kneeling beside the unconscious Lieutenant and Ezra was beside the Sergeant. With a nod to one another, they began stripping the prone forms of their uniforms as Elena hustled the girls into the back room. When the soldiers were disrobed, retaining only their underdrawers, they bound their feet and hands and stuffed their mouths with gags, then Gabe and Ezra rolled them up in the blankets and with a quick glance around, took the big burritos to the pack animals. Wolf had been standing watch and sniffed at the unusual bundles, then looked up and down the roadway as the men worked.

Once the two were firmly secured over the panniers on the pack animals, looking like a large bedroll or a bundled bunch of gear, Gabe and Ezra mounted up and started down the narrow alley behind the cantina, the big black wolf leading the way. Within moments, they were free of the *villa* and turned north to retrace their route toward the long mesa. Gabe repeatedly stood in his stirrups and searched their backtrail as they followed the ancient trail to the crossing near the confluence of the Rio Grande and Rio Chama.

It was less than five miles and a half hour when they neared the crossing. Moonlight danced off the ripples and the gentle gurgle of the waves was enticing. But the men did not hesitate and pushed the horses into the murky waters and were soon across. Another backward glance showed no pursuit but they pushed on, planning to be around the point of the mesa and into the flats soon. Three miles brought them to the mesa and the trail around the point. As they followed the ancient path, Gabe remembered their first encounter with the Apache when he and Ezra were on the far side of the river and the Apache were on the shoulder above them. A quick glance upward showed nothing and Gabe, somewhat relieved, nudged Ebony to a canter as they rounded the point of the mesa and took to the trail below the flanks of the long rise. When they neared the remains of the Escalante Hacienda, Gabe reined Ebony toward the ruins, stopped and swung down.

He looked at Ezra and said, "This is as good a place as any, ya' reckon?"

Ezra also stepped down, "Suits me. Prob'ly do 'em good to see what their friends have been doin'. Not that it'll do any good but maybe."

They loosed the bindings and pulled the bundles to the ground, heard grunts and moans as they landed, then started unrolling the blankets without showing any kindness. The two men rolled free, glaring at their two captors with anger flaring in their eyes until Gabe slipped his pistol from his belt and pointed it at the face of the Lieutenant. The officer glanced at the big wolf that stood, teeth bared and lip curling as he watched them, then back at Gabe, fearful of what he would do next. "I should just shoot you but I'm hopeful you might learn something from this." He jerked the gag from Delgado's mouth, waved the pistol in his face and shook his head to silence him, then with a knife in the other hand, quickly cut his bonds.

Ezra did the same with the Sergeant and the two men struggled to their feet, their bare chests and dingy underdrawers showing in the moonlight as both men stood wide-eyed before their captors. Gone was the arrogance and dignity that had been so much a part of the officer and the respect the Sergeant held for the Lieutenant had also waned. Gabe said, "We're gonna let you go now but you might want to look around. You see this hacienda? It had a family with twin daughters and hopes and dreams for their future. They built a nice home and rancho but your friends, the Apache, did this after they ruined the daughters! All because the likes of you were willing to trade guns for captives."

"What about our uniforms?" barked the Lieutenant, trying to assume his air of superiority as he glared at his captors.

Gabe chuckled and looked at Ezra, "Do you remember where we put the uniforms?"

"Uh, no, don't seem to reco-member. I'm sure somebody'll find 'em and put 'em to good use, though," laughed Ezra.

Gabe grew somber and looked at the two men, "Delgado," he began, intentionally avoiding the man's rank, "you used that uniform in a way it was not intended. You manipulated people, commandeered your personal wants, demanded subservience, all of which was not the purpose of the uniform. By any standards, you were a disgrace to the uniform. Without your rank and your position, you will find it much harder to make your way in this world. You just might have to earn or work for your needs."

"Well, we did send word to Pedro Vial and I'm sure he could use some day laborers to help him in his journey to the Pawnee," drawled Ezra.

"And I'm certain when you get back to Santa Fe, the governor will not restore you to the rank you held, nor you," Gabe added, nodding to the Sergeant.

"No one would blame us if we just shot you but that would be too easy for you," snarled Ezra, stepping back aboard his bay. He nodded to Gabe who stuffed his pistol in his belt and swung aboard Ebony. They turned away from the two barefoot men, waved to Wolf to scout ahead, and returned to the trail toward the mountains. They rode in silence for a short while but Gabe reined up, stood in his stirrups, and turned around, frowning as he looked back the way they came. "Hear that?"

Ezra had also looked back, "Yeah, war cries. Sounds like Apache."

"You don't suppose . . ." began Gabe as a grin began to split his face.

Ezra grinned, "Mebbe, I'd like to think so." He chuckled, turned around and dropped into the seat of his saddle, "C'mon big boy, let's head for home." The lead line to the mule and the piebald stretched tight as the long-legged bay stretched out on the dimly lit trail.

They rode into the night, eager to put distance between them and the settlements and anxious to see the mountains. They followed the little river that shadowed the ancient trail and when it turned north they remembered the route they followed when they traveled with Slow Turtle, the Caputa Ute. Steam from hot springs rose from the shadows to catch the moonlight and the travelers bypassed the inviting hot springs to keep to the trail. When the trail turned to the east, Gabe motioned Wolf to take the trail ahead and followed his friend along the dry creek bed.

Another couple miles and the trail moved due east where the dry creek bed came from the north. Gabe stopped, looking both ways and turned to Ezra, "Didn't we come from there?" pointing to the trail that flanked a long ridge and parted two low-rising ridges.

Ezra came alongside, looked at the distant shadows in the dim light, nodded, "Yeah, if you remember, we followed that long ridge below that flat-top. That little dry creek there meanders from high up to the north. That there's a mighty dry trail but the upper end has water."

Gabe looked at his friend, back at the trail, "Yeah, and that valley has lots of timber but at the upper end we take to the flats again. I remember." He looked back at Ezra, up at the stars and added, "Reckon it to be gettin' close to midnight, so as soon as we get into that valley and have some trees nearby, we prob'ly oughta stop and give the horses a rest, ya think?"

Ezra nodded, grinned, "Sounds reasonable," and nudged the bay to take the lead. Just the thought of home gave him renewed determination as he thought of Grey Dove and the kids. Gabe chuckled, knowing exactly what Ezra was thinking and grinned at the thought of his own family waiting. He nudged Ebony to follow the piebald as they took to the narrow and ancient trail.

31 / TRAVELING

It was late morning when Gabe rolled from his blankets. They had camped in the trees near the mouth of the long canyon that lay in the shadow of the long timbered ridge to the east. Uncertain as to their location, Gabe retrieved his scope from the saddlebags and with Wolf at his side, they left Ezra snoozing in the shade as they climbed the timbered slope to the crest of the long ridge. The spine of the ridge was limestone rimrock dimpled with tenacious piñon whose roots seemed to wedge through the smallest cracks in the hard stone, looking like spider legs that grasped the rocks to hold the scraggly trees in place. Scrub oak brush offered variety to the grey-green colors with their burnt orange and rusty leaves. Gabe walked parallel to the rimrock, searching for an access point until Wolf bounded between two piñon and mounted the ridge, turning to watch Gabe pick careful footing on the loose stone.

Atop the ridge, Gabe stood in the shade of a big juniper as he stretched and looked around. He looked to the eastern horizon to see the jagged peaks of the south end of the Sangre de Cristo Mountain Range and to the north stood the distant shadows of the remnants of ancient volcanoes, the ones they rode near on their journey south to Santa Fe. He slipped the scope from the case, stretched out and searched the flats that lay before them. As he scanned the plains, he saw a herd of pronghorns, a couple coyotes with heads hanging and tongue lolling after they lost a foot race with a jackrabbit, a couple dust devils, and rising heat waves. He looked up at the blazing sun, took another look at the distant isolated hills, and turned away to return to the camp. He caught the smell of smoke but saw nothing and knew Ezra was fixing his coffee but had built the small fire beneath the branches of the juniper so the smoke would dissipate and not give away their location. Gabe chuckled as he walked into the trees and stood at the edge of the camp, "Just couldn't wait, could'ya?"

"No need. I figgered you'd want some too, so here ya go!" answered Ezra as he poured both cups full of the steaming black java. They stood back from the fire as Gabe reported on his findings. "We're below that big flat we traversed on the way down, you remember where those solitary hills stood out like islands?"

"Yeah, so, we're makin' good progress then."

"Ummhmmm," started Gabe, looking up at the sun nearing its high point, "but that sun's doin' its best to discourage travelin' in the daytime but I figger we need to put a few more miles behind us, so . . ." he drawled as he took a big sip of hot coffee. "I'm thinkin' we could angle across the flats, split those hills, and make way to the Sangre de Cristo's. Then we can follow them north." He paused, glancing at Ezra and continued, "We can stop by those hills to camp, if need be, they're thick with timber and good cover. And if we want to rest a spell and continue in the night, we can do that too."

"So, what'chu thinkin', 'bout another week to get home?"

Gabe pursed his lips, nodding his head, "Yeah, 'bout that."

"Then let's get across those flats 'fore that sun cooks our noggins!" declared Ezra, finishing his coffee and pouring out the dregs.

It was late afternoon on the fourth day out of Santa Cruz when they neared the massive granite-tipped peaks of the Sangre de Cristo Range. Just south of those towering sentinels, the mountain range cradled a low saddle that birthed a pair of streams straddling a smaller handful of foothills. But Gabe and Ezra were bound to the north and eagerly sought refuge from the afternoon's sun in the shade of the towering ponderosa. With a short breather, they pushed on, staying within the trees, and looking for fresh water.

They bypassed a rocky draw and mounted a wide alluvial dome, the deep cut above that scarred the mountain slope promised a good stream and when they heard water, the horses picked up the pace, rounded the crest of the dome and dropped into some tall ponderosa. The crashing of water cascading from the high country and making its way below was what they wanted to hear and they glanced at one another, smiling broadly. The mountain stream was clear, cold, and noisy and most of all, inviting. The horses were quick to find a spot for their noses as Gabe and Ezra slid to the ground, anxious for a cold drink.

The last two days had been hot and dusty, the lather on the horses was caked with dusty mud, the sweat down the back and on the necks of the men was nothing but gritty grime. Gabe took his hat off and buried his head in the water, coming up laughing and water streaming from his hair and down his neck. He stood and went to the horses to begin stripping off the gear. The men led the animals into the water, dropped their leads and began washing them off with hands full of buffalo grass. The animals enjoyed the attention and the cool water but soon tired of the grooming and began looking for graze. A wide grassy shoulder invited the animals and all five were soon contentedly grazing.

Ezra said, "Unless I miss my guess, that roarin' comin' from up in them trees is a water fall and that's just what we both need to get rid of a couple day's dust!"

Gabe grinned, "You go on and have at it. I'll stay here and mind the horses and such."

Ezra laughed, "You don't have to tell me twice! Oh, and while you're at it, some hot coffee'd taste mighty fine after I have my bath."

Gabe laughed, shook his head, "Will that be all, sir?"

Ezra adopted a smug expression, pursed his lips, and answered, "For now, for now." Both men laughed and Ezra grabbed his clean duds and a blanket for a towel and started uphill beside the stream. When both men had finished washing and changing, the refreshed pair began preparing things for the meal and Gabe said, "You know, there's probably some deer, maybe some bighorns around, so, I think I'm gonna see if I can find some fresh meat."

"You go right ahead, I'm gonna fix that coffee you neglected and maybe get some biscuits in the pot," answered Ezra.

Gabe laughed, "You do that, dear!" and ducked when Ezra threw a coffee cup at him. He retrieved the Mongol bow from the gear, sat down to string it and once done, hung the quiver at his side and started through the ponderosa downstream. The sun was beginning to paint the western sky a bright orange and gold, bouncing the colors among the trees and bending lances of gold through the big branches. Gabe smiled, feeling especially good now that they were back in the mountains, breathing the pine-scented air and walking on pine needles and aspen leaves.

Movement caught his eye and he watched as several bighorn sheep came from the rocks on a narrow cliffside trail and picked their way to the water. Gabe stood still beside the big, white-barked aspen, its leaves fluttering in the early evening breeze. The thicket of aspen lay in the fold of the mountain and gave a brightness to the hillside, the matted leaves below giving Gabe quiet passage. He watched the dusty brown animals with their cream-colored rumps make their way to the stream, look around and dip their noses to the water, quickly step back and look around before taking another drink. A big ram with horns that made a full curl and more, strutted into the little clearing, the others stepping aside for him. Gabe counted five ewes, four lambs, and two young rams besides the big boss ram.

He watched as a few snatched mouthfuls of greenery and another drink and moved away for the others. The big ram was the last to drink and when he turned, the others started filing back toward the rocky trail. Gabe had nocked an arrow and stood behind the aspen but as the small herd started away, he slowly stepped from behind the tree, bringing the bow to full draw and sent the arrow whispering to its target. The black shaft pierced the low chest of one of the young rams who staggered a step, dropped to its knees, and fell to the side. The big ram made a quick leap over the downed animal and within seconds the entire herd was gone.

Gabe nocked another arrow, and slowly stepped close to the inert ram, nudged it with his foot and satisfied it was dead, he lay his bow aside and replaced the arrow in the quiver. He reached to his back and retrieved the larger of his Flemish knives in the sheath between his shoulder blades and knelt beside the carcass to start field dressing the ram. He paused, unmoving, listening. He felt, rather than heard something out of place, and the prickly feeling at the back of his neck told him something or someone was near. He flipped his knife and grasped the tip of the blade with his fingers, ready to throw. He slowly stood and turned, surprised to see an old man seated on a rock beside the same big aspen he had used to shield himself from the bighorns.

The man had wispy white hair that hung in braids over his shoulders, his dark skin was weathered and wrinkled, his buckskins were beaded and showed exquisite craftsmanship. He held a bow across his lap, his elbows on his knees and a broad smile split his face and danced in his eyes. He nodded, then with swift-moving hands and fingers, spoke in sign language. "That was a good shot with your bow. I have never seen a white man use a bow."

"You have seen many white men?" asked Gabe, also using sign.

"One or two, but none with a bow or that could sign."

"Is your village near?"

"My lodge and my woman are near. We are alone and hungry. You took my bighorn."

Gabe grinned, "I will share with you. My camp is near," nodding to the trees upstream, "you and your woman are welcome at our fire. We will have a meal together."

The old man grinned, nodded and started to rise. Gabe stopped him with, "Wait, I'll give you some of this meat to take to your lodge. Then you and your woman come to our camp and meet my friend and eat with us." The man nodded and watched as Gabe quickly cut a hind quarter free and lay it on the man's shoulder. He grinned and started through the trees, moving downhill beside the stream. Gabe quickly finished dressing the ram then, using the hide to carry the stripped meat, started back to camp.

32 / COMPANY

He dropped the bundle of meat on the pine needle carpet under the big ponderosa, chuckling as he turned to Ezra, "We got comp'ny comin' to dinner!"

"What?" blurted an astounded Ezra. "How is it that here in the middle of nowhere, hidden in the trees in the mountains, you find somebody to come to dinner?" He stood with hands on hips as Gabe laughed so hard he bent over. When he caught his breath, he stood erect and shook his head, "You look and sound just like my mother did when my father would bring someone home for dinner!"

"I ain't your mama!" grumbled Ezra. He shook his head as he lifted the lid on the dutch oven to check the biscuits. With a nod of satisfaction, he replaced the lid, added a couple more hot coals, then looked up at Gabe. "So, who's comin'?"

"Didn't get his name but I suspect he's Comanche.

An old man that went to get his woman and they'll be comin' along right soon."

Gabe had no sooner finished explaining when they heard, "*Marúawe!*" as the two visitors stepped through the trees. The old man led the way but held the hand of a tiny woman of about the same age. She had a fitted tunic over fringed leggings. The tunic had blue and white beading across the chest and down the arms accenting the fringe that decorated both. Her braided grey hair fell over her shoulders, almost to her waist, and a vermillion streak showed brilliantly at the part. Bright eyes danced with mischief and her step bewrayed her obvious age, although the weathered and wrinkled skin spoke of a long life lived. The man stepped forward and spoke in the tongue of the Comanche and sign, "I am Bear on Buffalo and my woman is Morning Light." The woman stepped close beside her man, looking wide-eyed at the shadowy wolf that lay just at the edge of the firelight.

Gabe began by speaking in the tongue of the Shoshone that he knew was similar to that of the Comanche but also used sign. "I am Gabe, Spirit Bear," and he nodded to Ezra.

Ezra stepped forward close to Gabe, "And I am Ezra, Black Buffalo," he paused, looking from Bear to Light, "Are you Comanche?"

The man's eyes widened as a slow smile painted his face. He glanced from the men to his woman, turned back to Ezra, nodded, "Yes, we are Comanche."

Gabe motioned for them to be seated on the lone log that lay at the side of the fire, seated himself opposite them and continued, "We come from the land of the Jicarilla Apache and Caputa Ute. We journeyed to Santa Fe for supplies. We are returning to our home and our families in the mountains to the north." He glanced from one to the other of the visitors, looking to see if they understood his sign and words. From his experience with the Comanche, he knew the language of the Shoshone and the Comanche were similar, yet each had its own dialect.

"We are *Widyu Nuu*, Sewing People, of the *Yaparuhka* band, Root Eaters, of the *Numunuu,* the people you know as Comanche."

"I spent some time with the *Yaparuhka* band, I know White Knife, Black Bear and Old Owl." As he spoke, he watched Wolf casually walk around the fire toward the tiny woman, who crowded close to her man, until Wolf lay down beside the end of the log, glanced up at the woman and lay his muzzle between his paws as he stretched out.

"We know those you speak of, but theirs is a different village." Bear paused, looked around and motioned to the wide valley below the tree line, "This was our summer camp several seasons ago. When we left our village, we remembered this place and time and chose to return."

"How long have you been here?" asked Ezra.

"We came in the time of greening," stated the old man, a wistful look glazing his eyes. His woman kept glancing to the wolf but did not appear frightened, just curious.

"We passed through this valley about that time when we were bound for Santa Fe. We traveled with a man and his woman from the Caputa Ute," explained Gabe.

The old man looked at his woman with a smile, then back to Gabe, "We remember." Morning Light looked at Gabe, then to the wolf and back at Gabe.

"He is our friend. He has been at my side since he was a pup. He knows you are friends and will not harm you. If you want to touch him, let him smell you, then you can stroke his scruff and behind his ears."

She smiled, glanced to her husband, and scooted a little closer to Wolf, who lifted his head, and appeared to smile at the woman. She held out her hand, let him sniff, and as she carefully and slowly stretched to touch him, Wolf lowered his head and let her feel his fur. She stroked his scruff and smiled up at Gabe and looked back to Wolf. They had made friends.

Gabe glanced to Ezra as he uncovered the dutch oven to check the biscuits. He nodded to Gabe, sat the lid slightly askew of the pot and used a stick to uncover several timpsila roots from the coals. He reached back for the trenchers, carved wood platters, and grabbed one of the willow withes that held the hot broiled strip of backstrap, put it on the plate, added a timpsila and a biscuit and handed the plate to the old man. Within moments, all had a plate before them and Gabe bowed his head and said a quick prayer of thanks and, with a smile to their visitors, started eating.

There was little conversation while they ate, the hot food and coffee especially enjoyable with the last of the orange and gold sunset faded to a mere hint of what it was, a cool breeze that whispered through the pine boughs, and the beginning of night sounds. When they finished and sat their plates aside, Morning Light asked, "You said you have families, are they like you?"

Gabe grinned, knowing her question was if their wives were native or like them. "Both of our wives are Shoshone. My woman, Cougar Woman, is of the Tukkutikka band."

Ezra spoke up, "And my woman, Grey Dove, is of the Kuccuntikka band."

"And do you have children?" she asked, smiling, as she voiced the concern of women everywhere.

"We both have two children. Black Buffalo has two boys, and we have a boy and a girl. They are all small," he held out his hand at the approximate height of the oldest, "but growing fast."

Gabe looked at Bear on Buffalo, "The rest of your

people, will they come soon?"

Bear dropped his eyes, glanced at his woman, then looked up at Gabe, "No, they will not come. It is the way of my people when there is snow on the mountain," he tapped his head indicating his white hair, "and we cannot keep up with the others, it is best for us to go off by ourselves and not be a burden to the people." He reached for the hand of his woman as they smiled at one another, "We will spend our last days together." He lifted his head and slowly waved his hand around to take in the beauty of the mountains and valley and the fading light of dusk, "It is a good place to die."

Gabe and Ezra looked at one another, slightly shaking their heads, and Gabe asked, "You walked from your lodge to our camp, do you not have a horse?"

Bear on Buffalo grinned, "Our horse was old like us and did not last long."

"What about supplies, you said earlier you were hungry and needed meat, do you have other supplies?"

"Our Creator has supplied us what we need. What we had, we have used."

Gabe glanced to Ezra, saw him nod, and turned back to the old man as Ezra rose and went to the darker alcove of the camp. Gabe assumed a somber expression, his brow furrowed, "We need your help, if you can. When we were in Santa Fe, we traded for all the supplies we needed. But we ran into a little trouble with some renegade Jicarilla Apache. We got a horse and some extra supplies but that horse is not one to pack and we don't have another packsaddle. So, you would be a big help to us if you would take those extra supplies and that piebald horse there," nodding toward the flashy colored white and black stallion. "That horse belonged to the war leader of those Apache but he has crossed over and won't need him now and we've got more horses than we need. And him bein' a stallion, I don't want him around my mares back home." He was very serious in his expression and looked at the old man, ascertaining his understanding. The old man nodded and Gabe continued, "I'm not sure what all is in those bundles but maybe they'll help you and your woman. If these are to be your last days, they should be good days," he added, emphatically, to which the old man nodded his agreement. Gabe glanced at the old woman who was smiling broadly, her gratefulness showing in her eyes as she did her best to control her delight.

Ezra had bundled some supplies together, wrapped them in a couple of blankets and tied the blankets together to drape them over the back of the stallion. He led the horse toward the fire and the old man rose and walked close, reaching out to let the horse sniff him, then stroked his head. He leaned to the side to look at the lines of the horse, looked back at Gabe, "This is a fine horse, strong legs, good chest, a fine horse."

"Well, we are grateful to you for taking him. We just did not know what we would do with another stallion." He nodded to Ebony, "I've had that one for many years and he's my best friend and he wasn't too happy having another stallion along."

The old man smiled, nodding, and understanding. Stallions are like the boss bull in a herd of buffalo and have little patience with any interlopers. Having two strong stallions in such a small herd would result in many fights and one or the other being injured and Gabe did not want to betray the loyalty and friendship of his Ebony.

Bear on Buffalo went to one knee to let his wife step on the bent knee, using it as a step to climb aboard the piebald. When she was aboard, she leaned down and stroked the big stallion's neck, spoke to him, and sat erect, reins in hand. She smiled at her man, looked at Gabe and Ezra, "You are a gift from the Creator. I have asked the Creator to give us more days and He has used you to make our end of time honorable and good. We are grateful."

Gabe nodded, feeling a lump in his throat, and fought the rising of tears in his eyes. They watched the old couple leave the camp, taking the same trail to return to their lodge. Gabe looked at Ezra and saw the firelight reflected in his watery eyes and mumbled, "So, we're an answer to prayer. Ain't that somethin'?"

33 / HOME

"Where do you suppose all that sand came from? Couldn't be from the mountain, they ain't got much o' nothin' but rocks and there's more sand there than ten o' them mountains could hold," drawled Ezra, as they made a wide swing into the valley to avoid the massive sand dunes that lay in the shadow of the Sangre de Cristo Mountains.

"Dunno, maybe God just had a pocket full left over after he made the beaches by the ocean and decided to dump it here." Gabe chuckled as he recalled a time his family had gone to the lake and he played on the sandy shore. When he returned, he dumped out his pockets and had a pile of sand for the frog he had in his shirt pocket. He remembered chasing his sister with the frog and taking a licking with a wooden spoon for the doin' of it.

"You don't suppose this valley was a lake way back

when, do ya?" asked Ezra, surveying the wide valley that lay between the mountains of the range and the foothills on the west. "Looks too dry to have ever had anything but cactus and rattlesnakes!"

"I don't reckon. If this had been a lake, you'd think there'd be sand all along them mountains but it's just right there. But over yonder," suggested Gabe as he pointed to the flats off their left shoulder, "that's alkali and that's usually from where there's been a lot of water and it dried up."

"Hmmm, the wonder of it all," drawled Ezra, nudging the bay in the direction of the tree line at the skirt of dark green that fell from the high mountain range. They made a long day of riding, stopping mid-day for the usual breather for the horses and to put the feed bag on Ezra. By dusk, they made camp in the lee of the mountains, well in the tree line, and near the upper end of the long valley.

When they sat back for their coffee, Gabe said, "I'm thinkin' we might make it home on the morrow. If this is where I think we are, we'll drop into the valley of the Arkansas come mornin' and make it to the cabin 'round noon!"

Ezra turned to look at him, "And here I was thinkin' we had at least a couple more days to go! So, what made the difference?"

"When we came down from the north, we went on the back side of the mountains, remember?"

"Yeah, and that's where we picked up Slow Turtle and his woman."

"And we came into this valley back yonder where those hot springs were, right?"

"Yeah, so now we're headin' straight north and that'll put us into the valley of the Arkansas?"

"That's the way I figger it."

"Well that there plumb tickles my backbone! Tomorrow! We'll get to see the women and the little ones. If that don't beat all!" He chuckled a mite, drained the coffee from his cup and tossed the dregs, and grinned at Gabe, "Then I'm gonna hit the blankets so we can get us an early start and get home!" Gabe laughed at Ezra but felt the same joy and anticipation and did not hesitate to go to his blankets.

They lay in their blankets, hands clasped behind their heads as they looked to the starlit sky. The whisper of the night breeze in the tall pines was the accompaniment of the carol of the night hawks and cicadas. The far-off cry of a lonesome coyote seemed to resonate with the lonely men and Gabe smiled when the romantic's cry was answered with an invitation from another. Although the men lay on opposite sides of the low burning coals, their thoughts were much the same as both talked with their Lord, offering their thanks for the safe trip and their soon return to their families.

When the first light of morn made silhouettes

of the jagged horizon of the Sangre de Cristos, the men were starting into the aspen that promised a trail to the lower valley. Wolf led the way and they soon took to an ancient trail following a meandering creek to the northeast. Heavily timbered shoulders pushed into the narrow valley, some bordered by towering limestone cliffs. Spring runoff had cut steep creeks from on high but few still held water. After the trail stepped beside the creek, they rode the shoulder for just over two miles and a slight bend around a point of rocks revealed the fertile valley beyond.

When they broke from the narrow creekside canyon, Gabe motioned for Wolf to stay close and they reined up for Gabe to make his customary survey of the valley for any possible dangers. Ezra took the horses to water at creek's edge, while Wolf led the way high up on the shoulder of a nearby ridge. The rising sun had painted the wide fertile valley with a golden glow, and Gabe's quick scan showed nothing but a small herd of elk near the little river that came from the western mountains.

He wasted no time bounding down the hillside and with a broad grin, reported, "I could see the white cliffs by our cabin!"

Ezra laughed, "So, I'm guessin' you didn't see any hostiles waitin' to take our scalps?"

"If there were, they're hidin'!"

"Then let's make tracks!" declared Ezra as he swung aboard the bay and snatched up the lead to the pack mule.

They pointed due north, bound for the wide bend of the river that lay at the foot of the series of long finger ridges that pointed east from the granite-tipped peaks of the Sawatch Range on the western edge of the long valley. From the bend of the river, they would cross the low ridges, until they reached the fertile green flats that lay east of their valley.

It was pushing mid-day when they crested the last ridge and looked down upon their valley. The top of the cabin was obscured by the nearby trees and the shoulder ridge that lay behind it but the sight of the massive white cliffs and the pillars of rising steam from the hot springs told the men they were home. They took the trail that sided the upper meadow and chuckled when Ebony and the bay greeted the other horses with whinnies that brought them all to the fence. Within moments, they dropped off the shoulder and rode up to the edge of the corral that stood beside the tack shed and lean-to, and just away from the cabin.

Both women stood on the porch, watching the men come into view beside the corral, and the children took off running to greet their fathers. Smiling women stepped off the porch and followed the scampering youngsters. Gabe and Ezra, both sporting wide grins, swung a leg over their pommels and slid to the ground, just as the older boys wrapped their arms around their necks. Everyone was laughing and talking and hugging, savoring the moment of the reunion, until Gabe said, "Whoa now! We've got to get the horses tended to and the packs unloaded, so . . . who's gonna help?"

All the kids chimed in, "I will, I will," and reached for reins and packages. The families made short work of stripping the horses and mule, rubbing them down, and turning them into the pasture. With many hands to do the work, the packs and gear bound for the cabin were soon at least on the porch. Ezra asked, "So, whatchu got for a hungry man to eat?"

When the excitement waned and the meal was finished, the youngsters were quick to go outside and the two couples followed, taking a seat on the porch, coffee cups in hand. They sat quietly, enjoying the sounds of children playing, and Cougar Woman began, "We," nodding to Grey Dove, "were talking while you were gone and we agreed that we would like to stay here."

Gabe frowned, glanced at Ezra, and back to Cougar, "Stay here, what do you mean?"

"This is our home. We want to stay here, let our children grow up here."

Ezra fought to keep a stoic face as he glanced at Gabe, looked at the women and started, "Well, we've been doin' a little talkin' too. We found out some things in Santa Fe that might be the cause of some changes. It seems that the U.S. has bought up all the land we've known as the Louisiana Territory, or Spanish, or French, or whatever it's been called, and there'll prob'ly be settlers comin' into this land."

The women looked askance at Ezra, showing expressions of confusion and wonder. He looked at them, then to Gabe, "You explain it, scholar!"

Gabe raised his eyebrows, shook his head, and motioned for the women to follow him into the clearing where he found a large spot devoid of grass and such and picked up a stick. The children gathered around thinking there was going to be a game of some sort and the little ones clung to their mothers' tunics as they watched Gabe begin. He started drawing in the dirt and made a crude map of the central portion of North America.

He pointed to the far side, "Now this is what is called the United States of America. It goes from the Atlantic Ocean, all the way over here," as he made a squiggly line from the top to the bottom of his drawing. "This is the Mississippi River. Now all of this," motioning to the land west of the big river, "is wilderness. It's been called French Louisiana because the French," and was interrupted by the oldest boy, "Are they a tribe?"

Gabe chuckled, "Yes, you might say that." And he continued, "They owned it. That why we met French traders and the traders from Hudson's Bay. But the Spanish, like those we ran into up north a ways, liked to think they owned it. But the French sold it to these people," he jabbed his stick in the eastern half. "So now, all of this," and he drew a diagonal line across the western portion from the top left corner to the Gulf. "is open to these people coming to this land and make homes and farms and such."

Cougar frowned, "But this is the land of the native people. Would they take it from us?"

"That might happen but there is so much land, and so few people, I don't think we need to be too concerned about that," he added. Yet he knew, in his heart, that no matter how vast the land may be, there would eventually be many people from the east that would come to this country and try to take it for themselves. He shook his head at the thought, stood and looked around the circle at the extended family.

"So, we've talked about it and we think it would be a good idea for all of us to stay right here and make a good home for all you youngsters to grow up and become great men and women!"

The women and children stood quiet, frowning, then slowly looked around to one another as smiles began to split faces and brighten eyes. And they hugged one another, the women, laying their heads on the men's shoulders, were especially pleased at the promise of a long and wonderful life together.

A LOOK AT: TO KEEP A PROMISE

The power of a promise made and a promise kept is realized when Jeremiah Thompsett comes of age and accepts the responsibility of fulfilling his mentor's long-held dream. Raised by an escaped slave in the midst of the Arapaho nation in the Wind River mountains, he now must track down the slave catchers that killed his adopted father and stole their cache. The Vengeance Quest takes him and his companions through the mountains and across the nation to fulfill the promise of freeing the family of slaves held dear to his mentor and adopted father.

Accompanied by Broken Shield and Laughing Waters, his Arapaho friend and his sister, the trek through the mountains and to Fort Union is fraught with hazard and ambush. It is here he is joined by Scratch, the crusty mountain man who joins him on his journey downriver and across country to find Ezekiel's family and to seek to free them.

ABOUT THE AUTHOR

Born and raised in Colorado into a family of ranchers and cow-boys, B.N. Rundell is the youngest of seven sons. Juggling bull riding, skiing, and high school, graduation was a launching pad for a hitch in the Army Paratroopers. After the army, he finished his college education in Springfield, MO, and together with his wife and growing family, entered the ministry as a Baptist preacher.

Together, B.N. and Dawn raised four girls that are now married and have made them proud grand-parents. With many years as a successful pastor and educator, he retired from the ministry and followed in the footsteps of his entre-preneurial father and started a successful insurance agency, which is now in the hands of his trusted nephew. He has also been a successful audiobook narrator and has recorded many books for several award-winning authors. Now finally realizing his life-long dream, B.N. has turned his efforts to writing a variety of books, from children's picture books and young adult adventure books, to the historical fiction and western genres.